It simply could not

Kitt looked down at the four-year-old girl beside her. With fresh eyes, she noted the child's dark hair lying in a familiar pattern. The perfect little nose with its faint sprinkle of freckles. The full mouth…

No! Kitt pushed the idea away. Mark would surely have told her if he had a daughter, for heaven's sake. He was the most honest man Kitt knew. So what if this child's father was also a reporter for the *Dallas Morning News*? Mark surely wasn't the only journalist here to cover the Fourth of July celebration on the Mall.

"I want my daddy now," the child said to her aunt, the young woman standing on her other side.

"I know you do, sweetheart." The woman bent to kiss her niece, then looked up at Kitt. "I've paged my brother twice. Mark should be here soon."

Mark!

Dear Reader,

When I visited Washington, D.C. (and nearby Alexandria, Virginia) I was enchanted by the magical mix of permanence and dynamic change that I found there. I loved the museums! The art! The historic buildings! But most of all I loved the people. There is something enthralling, electrifying, about a place where movers and shakers converge to shape a nation's destiny. It seemed the perfect setting for characters as bold and confident as Kitt Stevens and Mark Masters.

But even the boldest and most confident among us occasionally experience the feeling of not measuring up, of being "not good enough." We all have days when we think we're not pretty enough, or smart enough, or strong enough. Maybe we disappoint an employer, a friend or a loved one.

But the worst form of unworthiness is the feeling that we've failed ourselves.

You hold in your hands the story of one woman's triumph over that form of unworthiness. Kitt Stevens had to make a hard choice that left her disappointed in herself. And because of that choice, Kitt doesn't believe in love anymore. She doesn't think she deserves love. She even believes she's unworthy to mother a child. But through the steadfast devotion of a very special man named Mark Masters, Kitt learns to believe again—not only in herself, but also in the power of true love. I hope you enjoy Kitt's journey.

Darlene Graham

Your kind comments about my books are always appreciated. Visit my Web site at http://www.superauthors.com or write to me at P.O. Box 720224, Norman OK 73070.

This Child of Mine
Darlene Graham

HARLEQUIN®

TORONTO • NEW YORK • LONDON
AMSTERDAM • PARIS • SYDNEY • HAMBURG
STOCKHOLM • ATHENS • TOKYO • MILAN • MADRID
PRAGUE • WARSAW • BUDAPEST • AUCKLAND

ISBN 0-373-70958-7

THIS CHILD OF MINE

Because this is the story that first brought us together,
this book is dedicated with deep appreciation
to my very fine literary agent, Karen Solem.

CHAPTER ONE

KITT STEVENS was looking for a man.

But that wasn't what brought her up short, thinking, Who is *that?* as she stood in the enormous Corinthian-style doorway, where she had been halted by an uncharacteristic twinge of self-doubt.

The man who'd caught her eye—handsome, young, virile looking—was definitely not the man she was searching for. For a whole lot of reasons. And as soon as that thought flitted across her mind, the memory of the worst day of her life flashed up right along with it. It always happened like that: handsome man; worst day. Like some Pavlovian response or something.

Kitt reminded herself that she needed to stay focused. Her fiercest opponent was prowling around this room, probably at this very moment undermining all that she had worked toward in the past six months. Even so, her eyes strayed back to the good-looking man hovering around the food tables. He was still watching her.

But the nervousness she felt now wasn't the result

of the intense gaze of an incredibly handsome man—
Kitt got looks like that all the time, and dealt with
them—and her unease wasn't because she still felt
out of place at these stuffy congressional receptions,
even after a year in Washington. It was Marcus Masters—a man she'd never met—who daunted her. His
power. His wealth. His influence.

She tossed her silky reddish-blond bangs aside,
cranked her confidence up a notch and stubbornly
reminded herself that even if she didn't have the ad-
vantages Marcus Masters had, she *was* a good lawyer, and a good fighter, too. And, furthermore, she
reminded herself, the cause she was fighting for was
a critical one. Marcus Masters, powerful or not,
would simply have to be neutralized.

She stepped inside. People in impeccable business
attire, squawking like geese, milled about among the
heavy Federalist furniture and plush Oriental rugs.
Classical music tinkled down from speakers in the
high ceiling, melting into the heated conversation below.

To Kitt's right, heavy drapes were drawn back
from ten-foot-high windows, revealing the Washington Monument in the distance, shrouded by a haze
of summer heat and lit to a Titian glow by the sink-
ing sun. The stunning view gave the country girl in
Kitt a tiny thrill.

To her left, tables overflowed with exotic hors

d'oeuvres, while waiters swooped around the room with trays of drinks. Lauren had outdone herself.

"Kitt! You're finally here!" Lauren rushed up and caught Kitt's elbow. "Jeff predicted you'd do your workaholic act and miss all the fun."

Fun? Lauren, honey, Kitt wanted to say, *if standing around eating the same old finger foods, talking to the same old politicos, is your idea of fun, then you really must acquire a life.* Lauren Holmes, a devoted congressional staffer who spent her days—and often her nights—charging around the bowels of the Capitol in sensible shoes, was a fine one to lecture Kitt about workaholism.

Maybe Kitt had been in Washington too long— the polished lobbyist side of her emerged too easily: "I wouldn't miss your little do for anything." She jerked her head toward the extravagant spread, but didn't permit herself another glance at the handsome man. "I thought this was supposed to be a simple ice-cream social for the congressman's new interns."

Lauren shrugged. "Hey. If the broadcasters' association lobbyists want to pay Ridgeways to cater this deal, Wilkens isn't gonna say no. Like I keep telling you, this is Washington, not Oklahoma."

Ain't it the truth, Kitt thought. One thing she had quickly learned, in Washington words did not carry the same meanings as they did back home. In this town, *simple ice-cream social* meant *elaborate cocktail party.*

"You know the ethics rule." Lauren made quote marks with her fingers. "As long as the lawmakers are standing—"

"They can feed at the trough all they want," Kitt injected. She heaved a theatrical sigh, mostly to relieve her tension. "So ridiculous."

"You're just jealous because your organization can't afford to feed the hogs. Be grateful I got you in here."

Kitt smiled at her. Lauren and her friend, Paige Phillips, were the two best roommates on the face of the earth, and Lauren also happened to be the closest connection to Congressman Wilkens. "I am *extremely* grateful. And I'm grateful to Jeff for letting me know that the enemy's inside the perimeter. All I want is a chance to take one peck at each congressman or senator." Kitt pointed her slender index finger. "One tiny sentence, one *word* before Marcus Masters completely corrupts them with his buckets of money."

Lauren squeezed Kitt's arm. "So behave. And look!" She signaled a waiter. "There is actually some token ice cream." Then Lauren turned away to greet someone else.

The waiter lowered a hammered-silver tray bearing tiny waffle cones filled with every imaginable flavor. Kitt declined with a raised palm. Not that "Kitt the stick," as her brothers called her, needed to watch her weight. Ice cream was just too messy to permit the kind of maneuvering she needed to do.

She hailed a different waiter and lifted a stem glass of French limewater instead—alcohol was also inadvisable—then scrutinized the crowd again.

There were a few lawmakers, all from Wilkens's committee. A few exhausted-looking staffers. Some eager-looking interns. But mostly, there were sharp-eyed lobbyists like herself, including, of course, those who'd bankrolled this bash.

And, of course, the handful of beauty queens. One in particular was surrounded by a little cluster of power-suited men, all jockeying around the couch where the leggy young woman sat holding an ice-cream cone. Kitt sighed. *Washington.*

"How'd she get invited?" Kitt mumbled when Lauren turned back to her.

Lauren rolled her eyes. "Marcus Masters brought her."

Kitt's radar zoomed up. "Figures. Which one is Masters, by the way?"

"I have no idea what the old man looks like. Maybe he's one of the multitude worshiping at the Shrine o' Trisha. Look at her," Lauren's voice lowered, "perched on that divan like Scarlet O'Hara at Twelve Oaks. How does one woman, just sitting there eating ice cream, summon that much male attention?''

Kitt gave her friend a sarcastic smirk. ''Could it have something to do with that teeny skirt, those mile-long legs and those five-inch heels? Just a wild guess.''

Lauren rolled her eyes. Short and full-figured, Lauren had to fight the battle of the bulge every day and she would look absurd in five-inch heels.

Kitt jammed one hand into the pocket of her tailored slacks and congratulated herself because she'd abandoned such feminine tricks long ago. Ever since—why did she always think about that time of her life at highly charged moments like this? She reminded herself that, though it had cost her dearly, her mistake had at least expunged Danny from her life.

''Even the men not in her immediate orbit,'' Lauren mumbled, ''are glancing at her from across the room. *Trisha Pounds*. Irk. Even good old Jeff and Eric look—''

''Struck stupid.'' Kitt watched her two friends as they craned their necks to hear Miss Trisha's comments.

Kitt aimed the rim of her glass at the cute guy by the food tables. ''Well, at least there's one man who seems unimpressed.''

Someone had grabbed Lauren's arm, diverting her attention again.

The man by the tables was, Kitt decided, handsome enough to have any woman he wanted. In fact, Kitt noticed that Trisha kept glancing at *him*. Kitt smiled. The way he piled hors d'oeuvres on his plate reminded her of something her brothers would pull.

"That one looks more interested in the shrimp," Kitt muttered when Lauren turned back to her.

"Men and their prime directives," Lauren conceded. "Sex and food." Lauren squinted toward Trisha. "I kinda wish I could carry off the short skirts and spiked heels—" she dropped her voice below the din of conversation "—'cause I'm sure not having any luck finding Mr. Right. I mean, not that twenty-five's over the hill—but an occasional *date* would be nice." She sighed. "All the guys I meet are so…geeky."

Kitt listened to Lauren's familiar lament with one ear while she searched for Masters. Her eyes trailed back to the young man at the food tables. Too young, of course. And what a stupid tie—Mickey Mouse? Probably an intern. His jaws worked like a chipmunk's, bulging as he stuffed in shrimp. As if instinctively aware of being observed, he stopped midchew and shot Kitt a look with deep-set eyes that seemed to penetrate like lasers. His thick black eyebrows formed a sharp chevron for a millisecond, then he looked away and resumed chewing.

Lauren saw the exchange and elbowed Kitt. "Would you like to meet him?"

Kitt groaned. Lauren's relentless pursuit of Mr. Right—one for each of them—was wearisome. "No."

But Kitt felt herself blushing and took a quick sip of limewater to cool down, because the truth was, a bolt of electricity had coursed through her in that instant of eye contact. She sidled another look his way—he was assaulting the shish kebab this time—then she looked down into her glass again.

Definitely male-model material: neatly trimmed coal-black hair, square jaw, smooth tan skin. Tall. Built. And those eyes...

"Not only is he cute, that one is *rich*," Lauren was saying. "Boy, is he *ever* rich—"

Another staffer broke in and distracted Lauren with some crisis or other, and Kitt's gaze strayed once more.

This time *he* was studying *her*. Don't ever stare at men. That was one of Lauren's goofy rules for snagging Mr. Right. So, Kitt stared back.

When he didn't look away, Kitt felt forced to, frowning and brushing the lapel of her expensive silk jacket with the backs of freshly manicured fingernails. *You do not have time for pretty boys with challenging eyes,* she reminded herself. *Locate Masters.*

"Listen, I've gotta check on something," Lauren said. "Be good."

"I'll *try.*" Kitt sighed as Lauren rushed off. She brushed her bangs back, and braced one fist on her hip as she concentrated on the task at hand.

Congressman Jim Wilkens, the ostensible host and the one with the power over her precious media bill, was still hovering near the beauty queen. Kitt studied Wilkens over the rim of her glass. He was a tough one to figure. So far, Kitt and her contingent had convinced the congressman that a bill designed to protect children from unsuitable media influences would receive popular support. Wilkens, closely flanked by his aides, Eric Davis and Jeff Smith, didn't notice her, but Jeff mouthed "Hi," and Kitt gave him a little wave.

None of the unidentified men in the room looked the way Kitt pictured Marcus Masters—the obscenely rich, absolutely powerful California media mogul. She wished she'd had time to pull up a file photo before she left her office.

She sipped the limewater, and her stomach growled, reminding her that she'd skipped lunch again, so she made her way toward the crowd around the food tables.

Unfortunately, the feeding frenzy at the sumptuous

layout showed no sign of abating. Kitt had to squeeze into the only available space—near the fresh-fruit section of the buffet.

As she picked up an enormous strawberry, she *felt,* rather than actually saw, the man—the one who'd locked eyes with her—right beside her. Just as she lifted the strawberry, a tanned, muscular hand reached forward and their arms collided. The strawberry plopped into a dish of whipped cream, splashing a dollop onto Kitt's sleeve.

"Oh...I'm so sorry," he said, and grabbed her above the elbow. He snatched up a wad of paper napkins and started swiping at the sleeve.

"Gosh, I'm sorry," he repeated while the grip of his strong, warm fingers penetrated Kitt's sleeve and he succeeded in smearing the cream deeper into the delicate silk fabric.

Kitt, holding her plate aloft in the other hand, could only stare. Not at the fact that he'd made a mess of her brand-new lavender jacket. Not even at the fact that he'd grabbed her, a total stranger.

She stared at him because of the astonishing response she was having to his touch.

Shivers trilled up her spine, and she felt her face turning redder than the strawberries. And underneath the tailored lapels, underneath her modest white crepe blouse, underneath her sensible bra, her nipples had become as taut as rubies.

"It's…it's all right," she protested, and wriggled her arm from his grasp.

He dropped his hands stiffly to his sides, managing to smear whipped cream down his slacks in the process. "I'm really so sorry," he said as he grabbed more napkins and swiped at this new mess. "That's such a pretty jacket."

Kitt felt a split second of pity as she watched him fumbling with the napkins, then she quickly looked away, realizing she was staring at the front of a man's pants. "Don't worry about it," she said. She turned and made a dainty business of retrieving the fallen strawberry from the cream with a silver spoon.

"I was trying to get some more of those." He pointed at a tray of oval toasts topped with mounds of relish. "They're great." He was apparently attempting to smooth over his gaffe.

Without glancing up, Kitt said, "Yes, those are good. Bruschetta with goat cheese—a Ridgeways specialty. And they're very healthy."

"Shoot!" He snapped his fingers. "I was hoping they were *unhealthy*."

She peeked up at him then, and was caught off guard by the most divine, flirtatious smile she'd ever seen. Ever.

He wiped his hands and held up a cracker. "Now, why do you suppose they call these things Sociables? They don't seem all that friendly to me."

Good grief, Kitt thought. *Is he attempting to flirt with these goofy food jokes?* Kitt wasn't one to flirt. Deep inside she carried the scars of a relationship that had started out with flirting and ended in disaster.

When she glanced at him he quickly offered his name—"I'm Mark"—but not his hand. Maybe it was still sticky, or maybe someone had taught him at least that much etiquette—that you never offer your hand to a woman first.

Hearing the name Mark, Kitt felt her radar activate again, but dismissed the idea: *This couldn't be Marcus Masters. This guy's obviously a nervous Washington newcomer. And he's actually kind of sweet.* She gave him an indulgent smile and returned to selecting some strawberries.

"Well, uh—" he leaned forward "—let's see now. Do you come here often, and haven't I seen you somewhere before...or, were we soul mates in a past life?"

She glanced up, and there was that dazzling smile again. She revised her assessment. Maybe he wasn't so sweet. Maybe he was just another good-looking, arrogant guy on the make.

His grin froze in the chill of her silence. "Listen," he said. His eyes, she noticed just before he looked away, were intensely blue. "Would you let me at least pay to have your jacket dry-cleaned? I mean, if you'll give me your phone number, or I could give you mine—''

"Thanks, but that's not necessary," Kitt grabbed a napkin. "Excuse me, please." She walked away, never glancing back.

MARK MASTERS PRETENDED nonchalance as he finished wiping his sticky fingers. *Yessiree, that went real well.* The first time in ages he finds himself genuinely interested in a woman and what does he do? Slimes her sleeve and makes stupid jokes. He watched the slender blonde in the lavender pantsuit as she walked away. She stopped to make eyes at some tall, skinny guy. Great. She definitely had that Washington edge, but her blushing cheeks had conveyed a vulnerability, an…innocence that he found very appealing.

He looked toward the couch where Trisha Pounds, the gorgeous anchor from Channel 12, sat poised. Waiting, no doubt, for Marcus Masters's son to come and make his identity known. His father thought he and Trisha would make a "good match" and had chosen this opportunity to get them together. Mark would have to at least go and introduce himself. But eventually, Marcus Masters would have to give up running his son's life.

THE WHOLE ENCOUNTER with that young man had irritated Kitt, but it also intrigued her. Maybe it was those deep-set blue eyes. Vaguely like Danny's. To get her mind back on business, she sought out her friend Jeff, summoning him with an impatient jerk of her head.

Jeff Smith, Congressman Wilkens's aide—brilliant, sharp-featured—was thirty-five but retained the ranginess of a fifteen-year-old. He ran marathons a lot. He biked a lot. He cross-country skied a lot. He did everything an unattached and self-indulgent male could do to keep himself distracted from the basic superficiality of his life. And he worshiped Kitt. He bounded across the room in six lanky steps.

"You called, Your Ladyship?" He folded his long arms across his concave chest.

It was Jeff who had warned her that Masters might show up at this reception, smelling of money, competing for the congressman's favor, aiming to water down or even kill the new media regulation bill.

"Which one is Masters?" She didn't look at Jeff, continuing instead to check out the possibilities with sharp eyes.

"Marcus Masters, of Masters Multimedia fame?"

"No, Mohammed Masters, the waiter," she retorted.

"Kitt. Listen to me." Jeff spoke each syllable slowly, carefully, as if she had become suddenly addled. "Do not hook horns with Masters. That man will chew you up and spit you out."

"I've been chewed up and spit out for lesser causes. And I don't intend to hook horns or anything else. I just want to size up the competition."

Jeff sighed. "Have it your way, Joan of Arc. It just so happens I got introduced to Mark Masters right before you arrived."

"Great! Where is he?"

"Over there," Jeff inclined his head subtly toward the hors d'oeuvres tables where the young man, still glowing red, was standing alone, absently wiping his hands with some napkins.

Kitt was bewildered. *"Him?"*

"Yep. That's Marcus Masters."

"But that *can't* be Masters. He looks so...so *young*," she protested.

"Well. You don't exactly look twenty-eight yourself, sweetie, but that doesn't get in *your* way." Jeff poured on that adoring look that made Kitt squirm. She enjoyed Jeff as a friend, nothing more. "Who would guess that a cutie pie like you is actually a dangerous legal shark?" He batted his eyelashes.

Jeff could be such a sycophant. But he had a point. Not that she considered herself any kind of cutie pie, but she *was* kiddish looking. Who was *she*—with her size four figure, her freckles, and her bangs in her eyes half the time—to fault anyone for looking young?

"But...but *look* at him," she argued, mostly to herself. "That guy can't *possibly* have a multimillion-dollar media empire." Using Jeff as a shield, she peeked at him. The guy *did* have a fairly heavy five-o'clock shadow, and his shoulders were most impressive, but his face was as unlined as a statue of a Greek god. "That...that *kid* can't possibly be the one who wrote those huge checks to the congressman's campaign fund."

"Well, he is. That's Marcus Masters from Masters Multimedia in Los Angeles, California, developers of the promising—" Jeff cocked an eyebrow at Kitt "—well, some of us would claim, the *threatening*—LinkServe model."

Kitt felt a little clammy. A little ill. "Damn," she muttered.

"What's the matter, sweetie? You look like you ate a rotten mushroom."

"If only it had been poisonous."

Jeff responded to her melodramatics with a skeptical frown. "Come on. It can't be that bad."

"Oh, yes, it can." Kitt sipped the limewater, giving Jeff a pained look over the rim of the glass. "I just cut Mr. Marcus Masters, of all people."

"*Cut* him?"

Kitt nodded, looking around for a hole to swallow her up, or at least a handy couch to dive behind.

"*Cut* him?" Jeff repeated.

"Yes," Kitt hissed. "Blew him off. Gave him the cold shoulder."

"Cut him?" Jeff insisted on mocking her choice of words instead of sympathizing over the mistake she'd made.

"The guy tried to make conversation, tried to apologize for *this*—" Kitt waggled her stained sleeve "—and I gave him the Miss-Manners-Please-Excuse-Me-You-Clod treatment."

Jeff looked intrigued. "Why'd you do that?"

"He was flirting with me."

Jeff touched his long fingers to his lips in mock horror. "That cad!"

"You know what I mean. He was acting like some kind of stud, and I thought he was just another lowly intern or something. Look at him!" Kitt whined. "He looks like a…a kid!"

Jeff grinned. "And you crushed his poor little ego." He took a second to size up the younger man. "Well, if you rejected him, I guess I don't feel so bad about the heartless way you treat me. Why oh why do you do all this rejecting, Kitt dear?"

"Danged if I know." Kitt knocked her bangs aside with a punishing swat. But deep down, she did know. It was all mixed up, having something to do with her old anger toward Danny, and hence, toward all good-looking men.

Because he had no knowledge of Kitt's past with Danny—no one in her present world did—Jeff had his own theory. "I'll tell you why you do it." He tried to take her elbow, but Kitt shrugged him off. She headed for a couch by the windows to collect herself.

Jeff followed and continued, "You've never gotten over being the only girl stuck out on that farm with no mama and all those brothers picking on you day and night. Here. Sit." Jeff pressed her shoulder, lowering her to the prim little love seat. "Compose yourself. When you feel better, I'll introduce you to Masters."

"I think not," Kitt said, keeping her face turned toward the high window. She glanced at Jeff. "New plan. How long is Masters going to be in D.C.?"

Jeff walked around, seated himself facing Kitt, facing the room, and arranged his long legs as best he could in front of the spindly settee. "The grapevine says a week. Word is he actually drove here. Besides his interest in the outcome of the media bill, he has relatives in D.C. or something."

"A week! That doesn't give me much time. But, okay. Can you make sure Wilkens invites us both—me *and* Masters—to that dinner at Gadsby's next Tuesday? Maybe during dinner I can work in some facts about the bill, convince Masters it's not as big a threat as he thinks. And I'll pray that he won't remember this.'' She indicated the sleeve.

"I wouldn't count on that, sweetie." Jeff gave the room at Kitt's back a veiled glance. "He's checking you out right now. It'd be hard to forget your yard-long mop of red hair."

"My hair is *not* red! It's strawberry blond!"

Jeff raised a palm, grinning. "Hey! I'm not one of your ornery brothers. I happen to love your hair."

Kitt ran a hand through her bangs. "I guess I'll just have to…do something different with it." She stood up. "Just arrange that dinner, okay? Now, if you'll excuse me, I think I'll make my apology to Wilkens for cutting out early and then go dye my hair black."

Jeff smiled, assessing Kitt's burning cheeks. It wasn't at all like her to get so wrought up over a little social misstep. And it sure wasn't like her to miss the opportunity to work a room. "Go on," he said, waving a palm at her. "I'll tell Wilkens you got sick or something."

"And you won't be lying," Kitt sighed, and brushed her bangs back again. "Right now, I feel positively nauseated."

She straightened her jacket and made a beeline for the door, permitting herself one last furtive appraisal of Marcus Masters. He was across the room, getting introduced to Trisha Pounds. Kitt studied his broad back as he reached forward and took the beauty queen's hand. Who would have ever imagined this? That pretty boy is the media magnate!

CHAPTER TWO

DYEING HER HAIR BLACK might have been less expensive, and certainly less painful than this. The thing was called a cobra braid and was giving Kitt a headache before she'd even left the salon. But the elaborate swoop of braids was not meant to be comfortable, or even flattering. It was meant to drastically alter her appearance for tonight's dinner at Gadsby's Tavern.

And it certainly did the job. It was such a radical change from her blunt-cut mane and wispy bangs off a side part that Kitt found herself repeatedly checking the rearview mirror on the way home. Even the *color* of her hair looked different. The foreign hairdresser had kept patting it. "Thees braids you can shawmpooo and keep, yes?" Delightful news, Kitt thought, since she already wanted to rip them out.

She had dressed carefully. "Elegant casual" is how Lauren described her sleek black pantsuit, creamy silk shell and demure pearls.

The two-hundred-year-old town house that Kitt shared with her roommates, Lauren and Paige, who also worked on the Hill, was within walking distance of Gadsby's. She decided to save herself the frustration of hunting for a parking place in crowded Old Town.

The oppressive midday heat had subsided, and she drew in a deep breath, savoring the oily sweet scent of colonial boxwood, a fragrance she loved, along with everything else about historic Alexandria, Virginia. The hand-lettered wooden signs hanging at right angles over the antique shops. The softly glowing colonial-style street lamps. The brick sidewalks and cobblestone streets. All this quaint charm only six miles from the gritty hustle and bustle of urban D.C.

She brushed the top of a boxwood hedge with her fingertips as she mapped out her strategy for the evening—convincing Marcus Masters that the new media bill posed no threat to Masters Multimedia. Convincing him, in fact, that adequate regulation would actually make his latest product easier to market. A tall order.

But Kitt loved a challenge, especially when it meant going up against good old boys like Marcus Masters.

"Go for the gonads, honey," she had often advised her grieving divorce clients back in Tulsa, where she got her start in the law firm of Kinser,

Geotch and Baines. The KGB of divorce firms, their opponents called them.

They'd stop sniveling then—those abandoned and abused and betrayed wives—and stare at her over their soggy shredded Kleenex. And then slowly, like a new day dawning, they'd smile. Kitt always treasured that first smile of recovery.

It was at KGB that Kitt discovered she loved to make the smiles of the underdog permanent, that she was good at defending the defenseless, that she could fight, when her clients wouldn't—couldn't—fight for themselves. And of course, it was there that she learned to go after the money. She got so skilled at it that male lawyers facing a messy divorce actually started retaining *her* to ensure that she couldn't go after *their* gonads.

She permitted herself a flicker of a smile at the memories, but nowadays she funneled all of that skill and energy into championing the Coalition for Responsible Media. Unlike divorce law, she found her new work—lobbying for an organization that was trying to enact sensible controls over the media— uplifting.

She rounded a corner and Gadsby's Tavern came into view. An ancient narrow three-story facade, it housed a museum and one of the finest restaurants in Old Town. Only the best for Congressman Jim Wilkens and crew.

She checked her watch, glanced up the sidewalk, and spotted none other than Marcus Masters, pumping coins into a parking meter beside a silver Lexus LS 400.

She watched his movements: a slight bend to his knees, his muscled shoulders and thighs bulging even in his tailored suit, his large hands depositing coins in the meter and turning the knob in one brisk motion.

Wow, she thought reflexively, then smiled. This was her chance to disarm the mighty Mr. Masters with a small kindness.

"In precisely two hours you'll have a big fat parking ticket," she said as she walked up behind him.

When he turned and frowned, Kitt felt her knees go a little quaky. Even frowning, he was extraordinarily handsome.

She inclined her head. "You're Marcus Masters, aren't you?"

"I'm Mark." He smiled and nodded. In the dusky evening light the white of his teeth and his shirt collar seemed to glow against his tan skin. She reached up to brush her bangs back before she remembered they weren't there, then brought her hand down to her side self-consciously.

"And you'll be joining Congressman Wilkens at Gadsby's Tavern?" she continued.

He nodded. "Have we met?" he said. "I'm sorry. I…I don't recall."

Thank heavens, Kitt thought. She extended her hand. "I'm Kitt…I'm a friend of Jeff Smith's. The congressman's aide?" This was true. She *was* Jeff's friend. Masters didn't need to know about her position at the Coalition for Responsible Media. Not yet.

He smiled broadly and Kitt was relieved to see no hint of recognition in his eyes. "Nice to meet you, Kitt," he said as he enclosed her hand in his firm, muscular, my-oh-my-so-very-warm one. In that instant of touch her eyes took in the immaculately trimmed nails, the few spiky dark hairs on tanned skin, the crisp white cuff. And in that instant she felt it again—the unmistakable and, for Kitt, dreaded, sexual electricity.

He released her hand, still smiling that wonderful smile. "I'm glad I'm in the right place. The streets here are…well…confusing to an out-of-towner."

"Yes," Kitt agreed, remembering her excuse for approaching him. "And you've only got two hours on that meter." She pointed. "They'll ticket you then. And tow you eventually. Alexandria cops don't care if it's a clunker or a Rolls."

"Oh, yeah?" He looked at the meter, then back at her.

He rubbed his square jaw, frowning most appealingly. "Then I guess I'll have to put more money in the meter later."

"Feeding the meter won't save you," Kitt advised. "Tell you what—" she looked at her watch "—there's time to walk over to the Ramsey House—the visitors' center. We'll get you an extended parking pass, since you have an out-of-state tag—" *His tag was from Oklahoma? That's odd.* But it would be imprudent to let on that she knew enough to ask, *Shouldn't it be California?* "The pass will let you park here as long as you wish."

Again, he smiled that gorgeous smile. "Thanks. That's really nice of you."

Kitt felt embarrassed by his gratitude, knowing her motive wasn't hospitality so much as manipulation. "It's just a couple of blocks. This way."

He jammed his hands in his pockets as he strolled beside her, appearing to observe his surroundings—and her—with genuine interest. "Old Town is really fascinating." He took in a huge breath as if trying to inhale the history. "Do you live here?" he asked.

"Down near the river, a few blocks." She pointed east.

"How do you like Alexandria?"

"It's charming. I guess Congressman Wilkens wanted to get away from the Hill tonight."

"Have you lived here long?"

As they walked and talked she realized that he had

a knack for open-ended questions that sounded simple, but that elicited more information than Kitt intended to give. By the time they'd completed their stroll to the Ramsey House, he'd discovered that she had lived in Washington less than a year, that she was part Irish and part Scottish, and that she was originally from a small town called Cherokee, Oklahoma.

But even when she mentioned her connection to Oklahoma, he didn't volunteer any information about himself or his Oklahoma car tag.

As they climbed the narrow flagstone steps to the garden in front of the Ramsey House, Kitt was ready to focus the conversation back on him.

"Tell me, how did you get to be such a force in the media at such a young age?" She glanced at him over her shoulder.

"A *force?*" He smiled crookedly at the mounds of colorful impatiens in the planter beside him. "I wouldn't say I'm any kind of *force* yet, but I'm working on it."

Kitt stopped in her tracks and looked down at him. A man who owned eighty-six diversified media companies, with almost two thousand employees, didn't consider himself a force in the media? His answer made no sense, but his demeanor seemed utterly sincere.

She studied the top of his dark hair while he

rubbed a tiny red flower petal between thumb and finger. "Working on it?" she said quietly. "That's an incredibly modest way to describe your position."

He raised his eyes. The devastating blue was shadowed with confusion, but otherwise his expression was as innocent and fresh as the garden around them. "Not really," he said. "I am just getting started." He turned his attention back to the flowers. "What're these called? They sure are pretty."

She was so stunned by his comment—*just getting started?*—that she simply answered distractedly, "New Guinea impatiens," as she watched his strong fingers caressing the delicate petals.

He squinted up at her. "Do you always wear your hair like that?" Another question out of the blue, this one troubling.

"No." She blushed and touched her hair, worrying that he was remembering her as the rude woman at the hors d'oeuvre table the other night.

But he only smiled. "This garden is really neat," he said.

"Yes, it's lovely." She turned and proceeded up the steps, feeling unsettled. Marcus Masters was the most baffling man she'd ever met, and, Kitt noted, he had neatly eluded her original question.

Conversation on the walk back to Gadsby's consisted of Mark's polite comments about their charming surroundings and Kitt's knowledgeable responses. She told him about Georgian, Federalist and Victorian architecture. She told him about a ghost legend. She told him where the best restaurants were.

But the entire time, the conversation was overshadowed by Kitt's uncomfortable feeling that something about Marcus Masters did not add up.

And every time their eyes met, Kitt thought she might melt into the sidewalk. And for her, the chemistry between them was wholly unanticipated. Wholly unwelcome.

As they walked into Gadsby's, he said, "Let me guess. Federalist classical influence."

"Yes!" He certainly caught on quickly. "The symmetry reflects the conviction of that period that—"

"—there's order in the universe."

"Exactly," she said. "And see the bar? It's actually a small cage to keep the ruffians away from the hootch. Hence the term barkeeper."

"Neat."

The guy kept saying "neat."

And Kitt kept thinking, *Something's wrong.*

They wound their way through the tables in the taproom, then past smaller dining rooms painted in colonial colors to a private one, where, amid glowing candles and dark plank flooring, they found the congressman's intimate party of eight.

Oh dear, Kitt thought. *The walk to the Ramsey*

took longer than I calculated. The waiter was already opening a second bottle of Pouilly Fuisse Latour. But no one, least of all the congressman, seemed perturbed at their tardiness. In fact, Marcus Masters was greeted effusively, like some long-lost son.

"Mark! Glad you made it!" the congressman said as he stood. "It looks like you've already met Kitt." He gave her a passing smile, then grabbed Mark's elbow and introduced him to the others at the table.

Kitt was determined to keep a low profile until she saw the right moment to make her point. She tried to seat herself quickly, but Mark dashed around the table to hold her chair, then he sat directly across from her, boring a hole through her with those blue eyes. Kitt's pulse raced. She decided to skip the wine.

So did he, she noticed.

Her uneasiness persisted while salad was served and even as they nibbled on George Washington roast duck. A lute guitarist plucked out period songs while Congressman Wilkens dominated the table talk. The old man reviewed the latest controversy over violent and sexually explicit music, videos and Internet content, explaining the workings of the new media regulation bill intended to address the problem.

Preaching to the choir, Kitt thought. She, in particular, knew these arguments by heart. She had constructed most of them. Wilkens was obviously yak-king for Masters's sake. Trying to convince him that the bill was fair, so Masters wouldn't turn his money toward defeating it…and by extension, the congress-man.

She tried to relax, happy to let Wilkens do the talking. But she cringed a bit every time her pal Jeff opened his mouth, even though she'd warned him not to betray her connection to the Coalition for Re-sponsible Media. A couple of times she caught her-self touching her weird braids and she swore Masters glanced at her when she did. He gave her a funny little look. Almost…amused, and it made her jumpy.

Otherwise Masters said nothing, looked gorgeous and shoveled in food. Only when he'd scraped the last crumb of English trifle from his dessert plate did he lay aside his fork and speak. Not to the congress-man. To Kitt.

"Tell me, Ms. Stevens," he said, nailing her with those intense blue eyes, "why doesn't the Coalition for Responsible Media expend its energies *support-ing* technologies like LinkServe instead of trying to undermine LinkServe's efforts to give consumers more choices, more control, more freedom?"

What? Kitt stared at Masters and blinked. But be-fore she could rally from realizing that Mark Masters knew exactly who she was, what she was doing here, why she had been so helpful about parking meters and so informative about period architecture, Congressman Wilkens jumped in and multiplied her shock and disorientation tenfold.

"Now, Mark," he said, "I'm sure we can come up with a compromise that encompasses all interests, consumer protection, First Amendment rights and your father's favorite, free enterprise."

"His *father?*" Kitt mouthed and sent Jeff—who looked as if he'd been gut-shot—a stare that asked the obvious question: Is this *the* Marcus Masters or not?

Yes and no, it seemed. Kitt swiveled her head in Masters's direction while the congressman blathered on.

"I only wish your father could have stayed in D.C. a little longer while we hash this thing out. But then I suppose you're the next best thing. His representative, as it were."

The old congressman, for some strange reason, grinned and winked at Kitt. As if she knew what the hell was going on.

"His representative?" Mark Masters said. "Hardly, sir." He tossed his napkin beside his plate. "I'm pursuing my own goals here. I don't work for Masters Multimedia anymore and I don't think I would be a very good intern to you if I did." He steepled his hands above his plate and pressed his forefingers to his lips as if to indicate he'd spoken his piece.

The congressman's grin faded. He cleared his throat. "What do you mean, you don't work for Masters Multimedia anymore? What about your Link-Serve model?" he said.

Masters's dark eyebrows knit together. His deep blue eyes glinted with something Kitt couldn't identify. Determination, perhaps, or...defiance. He lowered his hands before he spoke. "After I developed the prototype, I turned LinkServe over to my father for testing. In the Florida market, I think."

Wilkens seemed surprised, even disappointed by this announcement. "Really?" he mumbled.

Kitt wondered fleetingly if Wilkens was playing both sides of this issue: Masters for the money, the CRM for the consumer votes. *Great.*

One of Wilkens's female aides piped up. "How exactly would LinkServe work, Mark? I mean..." She faltered as Masters turned the full force of those blue eyes on her. "I mean...what will it do, exactly?"

The main thing it will do, Kitt thought, *is make Mark Masters even more hideously wealthy than his old man.*

Masters smiled that luminous smile at the aide. "Think of LinkServe as a multimedia communications system—your telephone, your TV, your computer, your best friend's face. All coming to you over one neat, *linked* communications—" he hesitated here, apparently searching for the perfect word "—box to serve you." Then his smile expanded. "LinkServe," he summed up.

"Wow," the aide said, and Kitt wondered if the woman was "wowing" over the technology or the blue eyes.

The congressman leaned forward, frowning now. "Pardon me for asking," he said, "but I must know. It was my understanding that you kept your percentage in LinkServe?"

"I've retained some interests, but only for as long as I'm in college. I assure you, sir, I want to be treated like any other intern in your office."

The congressman hesitated, only for a heartbeat, but long enough for Kitt to pick up on his very real discomfort with this young man's unexpected declaration of independence. "Well, of course, of course," he said. "Just because you're Marcus Masters the Third doesn't mean you're not like any other intern, here to learn about the legislative process." He leaned toward Masters confidentially. "And you shall. For example, I trust this dinner has been edifying?"

Masters relaxed back into his chair. "Yes, sir, it has. Working with lobbyists like Ms. Stevens here is exactly what I want to do." He turned a thousand-watt smile of perfect teeth on Kitt. It was the same smile that had looked so warm and benevolent earlier, except now it looked utterly feral.

Kitt managed a nod and a weak smile of her own. If she'd been broadsided before, she was absolutely flattened now. This man, this Marcus Masters the Third, had known exactly who she was and what she was up to the whole time he'd had her yammering about flowers and ghosts. The whole time he'd been saying "neat" like some kid at Disneyland. Had he known even back at the ice-cream social when he tried to flirt with her? Her cheeks flamed. *Do you always wear your hair like that?* Geez.

"Great!" Wilkens boomed, now that his own moment of tension with the younger Masters had passed. "I have an idea. Why don't you spend some time with Kitt here, if that's agreeable to your people—" Wilkens shot Kitt a look that signaled she'd better play ball "—and get the CRM's take on this whole thing. Then write it up in a report for me by, say, the end of next week."

"*If* that's agreeable to Ms. Stevens." Masters smiled at Kitt again, and this time she swore his incisors actually looked pointier.

She swallowed, suddenly feeling like a scrawny chicken facing a wily fox. "Well," she stalled, "I'm afraid spending time at the CRM headquarters would be kind of…kind of…*dull* for Mr. Masters."

"Nonsense!" The congressman was still talking too loud. "It's the kind of experience Mark needs, distilling both sides of an issue for me." He looked magnanimously at Masters.

Mark held a palm up at Kitt in oath. "I promise I will state your case fairly and impartially to the congressman." His forehead creased sincerely.

Kitt had the queasy feeling she'd been outflanked. The feeling that her prey had suddenly become the predator, and a cunning predator to boot.

CHAPTER THREE

KITT PACED the length of her narrow third-floor bedroom and raked her hands through the weird ripples
the stupid braids had left.

Two stories below, she could hear Lauren and
Paige practicing their new vocal number. The three
women had formed a trio as a creative outlet and had
become quite popular at the church. But tonight Lauren's delicate soprano contrasted with Paige's athletic alto, and without Kitt's second soprano modu-
lating between them, they sounded strained. Kitt felt
a pang of guilt. She should be downstairs practicing.
But at the moment she could barely breathe, much
less sing.

She had beaten a retreat home from the disaster at
Gadsby's, carefully hung up her expensive black
pantsuit and proceeded to pace.

The memory of Mark Masters's face when he'd
asked her that pointed question about LinkServe, of
his fingers rubbing the flower petals, of the way he
ate, moved, used his hands, of his eyes, so blue and

deep-set, all of it played in her mind like images from some cheesy romantic comedy.

It couldn't be, just couldn't be, happening.

But she recognized the signs in herself already. Signs of…infatuation. And, to Kitt Stevens, having these feelings had once proved devastating. *Better not to even let anything start,* she warned herself. Love wasn't a fairy tale. Love meant entanglements, trouble…pain.

She could keep these feelings of attraction at bay, she reminded herself, if she kept her mind on her business. She marched to the bed, rummaged around in the covers, retrieved her portable phone and punched in a familiar number.

Jeff's nasal voice on the answering machine said, "Hi. Eric is out golfing, and I'm working like a slave. Leave a message." Kitt grinned because Eric's message was similar: "I'm killing myself for the congressman and Jeff's out barhopping."

"Jeff, pick up. It's me."

"Yes, my sweets," a live voice immediately answered. "I presume you called to crawl my ass about the Mark Masters screwup."

"Later. And while I'm at it, remind me to chew you out for talking so pretty. But first, tell me what you found out."

Jeff sighed. "It seems the younger Masters is Wilkens's intern from the University of Oklahoma.

Brilliant. Chose O.U. because of the Carl Albert Center.''

"The Carl Center?" Kitt muttered. "Where they do all that in-depth research into federal government operations? Is this guy some kind of policy wonk?"

"I guess. Of course, his father could send him anywhere, and tried to. But the kid, who's no kid, by the way, dropped out of U.C.L.A. the first go-round. Got in some kind of woman trouble. The old man, the real Marcus Masters, the one who's trying to control Wilkens, was only in D.C. for a day before he zipped out on his Lear.''

"Dang!" Kitt dragged her hand viciously through her kinky hair at that news. So, she'd missed her chance with Masters, and gotten the old man's son underfoot in the process.

Jeff went on in a rush, "I'm guessing the son is the relative I heard about. Sorry for the bad poop, Kitt. Old man Masters was supposed to be at that reception, I guess because his son was one of the incoming interns. But he didn't show. In fact, Trisha was really disappointed—''

"Trisha," Kitt injected.

"What have you got against her, anyway? She's really nice."

Kitt kept her thoughts to herself, but said, "Go on."

"Well, it turns out the old man wanted Mark to

meet her. She works for an affiliate owned by Masters Multimedia.''

Keepin' it all in the family, Kitt thought.

''Anyway, I promise, I knew none of this. I mean, I knew there were two interns who arrived late in the day that I didn't meet—we let Eric handle them— but I sure as hell didn't know one of them was Marcus Masters's son. I can't apologize enough for this mix-up. Kitt?…Kitt? Did you hear me? I'm really sorry.''

Kitt quit pacing and plopped down on the bed. Thinking. Scheming, actually. She didn't really hold Jeff accountable for this fiasco. He certainly had nothing to do with the congressman's bright idea to send Masters over to *her* turf. ''Don't worry about it,'' she answered. ''Send me some chocolates or a couple of tickets to Aruba or something.'' She yawned loudly into the phone. ''Listen, I'm beat. Thanks for checking the guy out. You and Lauren really should communicate more. Turns out she knew he was Marcus Masters's son the whole time.''

''Maybe *you* should communicate with Lauren more often,'' Jeff said. ''She's your roommate.'' His voice dropped to a seductive level. ''Hey. If I do send the tickets, will you take me to Aruba with you?''

Kitt raised the mouthpiece of the phone to her

forehead, rolled her eyes to the ceiling, releasing a slow hiss of impatience.

"Kitt? You there?"

Kitt lowered the phone. "I'm just tired, Jeff. I'll talk to you tomorrow. Meanwhile, I've got to figure out what to do with Mark Masters in the morning. Oh, by the way. I won't need a ride."

"Why? You braving the traffic?"

"No. After we left the dinner, when I was slinking home, Mark Masters caught up with me and offered to pick me up tomorrow."

"What on earth for?" Jeff sounded suddenly wary, maybe even a little peevish.

"I honestly don't know. Maybe he was just being nice. But I don't buy the I'm-Just-Here-To-Learn routine he handed the congressman."

"If he's Marcus Masters's son, you can bet he's after something."

"I can handle him." Kitt yawned again.

"Uh, yeah, if anybody can, you can. That's cool."

But Kitt got the feeling Jeff didn't think it was cool at all, and the truth was, neither did she. In fact, the whole idea of doing anything with Mark Masters, anything at all, felt vaguely...dangerous.

And that night, for the first time in a very long time, Kitt dreamed the old dream. The nightmare about her baby.

This time it came to her like a dream within a

dream. She was blinking at the golden shafts of evening sun that seeped through the bent miniblinds in her tiny student apartment at the University of Tulsa. It was late summer, when the university was as dead as a ghost town, and here she was, alone and heartsore.

She was curled up in a ball on her side, and, despite the oppressive Oklahoma heat, she pulled the comforter tighter around herself, like a cocoon, sealing the pain out...or sealing it in, she wasn't sure which.

All she wanted was sleep, but with sleep came the dream.

A dream that plagued her so much throughout her last year of law school that Kitt had worried that she might not have the strength to finish. But she couldn't—wouldn't—let Danny take that one hope away from her. Not after working so hard for so long. Not after only one mistake. All through that last year of school, the dream tormented her.

An infant—so small, so weak—clung to her, grasping with transparent fingers, floating from the filament of a tiny, reaching arm, surrounded by a soft white light.

But the baby always floated away. Each time Kitt reached out frantically to draw him back, he drifted farther. The child, she sensed, even as she dreamed, was forever lost to her.

Her baby.

Her endless nightmare.

Tonight she awoke in her Alexandria town house in a sweat, gasping. She sat up, switched on the lamp, stared down at the front of her T-shirt, half expecting to actually see something there. But the faded letters of a No Fear logo was all she saw. Shaking, she swung her slender legs over the side of the bed and scrubbed her hand over her face.

No fear indeed. Whenever the dream overtook her in the middle of the night, *all* Kitt Stevens felt was fear. Pounding fear. Fear that she had made the wrong decision. Fear that her baby was not all right.

During that time—four years ago now—that Kitt had decided she didn't believe in love. No, she'd told herself, she couldn't believe in love, never would again. She could believe in a lot of things—her faith, her friends, her ideals—but never love. That decision had been her only defense.

Love. Now she shivered at the idea.

Why had the dream returned now, when she'd thought it was all finally behind her?

CHAPTER FOUR

THE OFFICES OF the Coalition for Responsible Media
consisted of four cramped rooms at the top of three
flights of stairs in an ancient, crumbling nineteenth-
century building on the fringes of Old Town.

Enthusiastic volunteers teemed in and out of cu-
bicles crammed with file cabinets, beat-up desks,
computers and a perpetually zipping photocopier.

"Where do all these people come from?" was
Mark Masters's first question as he observed the bee-
hive of activity, already at a fever pitch at eight in
the morning.

Before Kitt could answer, a young man hailed her.
"Ms. Stevens, Senator Goins on line one."

She pushed her back-to-normal bangs aside, and
said, "Take a seat," to Masters without introducing
him to anybody. She had no intention of making this
guy too comfortable.

Then she got so busy bending congressional ears
that she didn't see him for the next hour. Which was
just as well. Their beginning this morning had been
rocky.

The first thing out of his mouth when he picked her up in the disgusting foreign Lexus was, "What a relief! I was afraid you'd still have your hair up in that snaky braidy thing."

Little snot.

Kitt had blushed at her own folly. The expense. The discomfort. For nothing. "Oh, you didn't like my wig?" she cracked as she settled herself into the leather seat.

He grinned as the precision engine purred to life. "You borrowed it from the *Star Trek* props room, right?"

Kitt pursed her mouth sourly. Normally, she loved this kind of repartee. With four brothers, she'd grown up on a steady diet of it. But from this man, it rankled. Because he'd known who she was the whole time, stupid hairdo or no stupid hairdo. Had he even known at the ice-cream social? Had he been mocking her instead of flirting with her? Pride prevented her from asking.

She looked over at him. Again, he was immaculately groomed in a navy-blue worsted-wool suit—the same tailored suit he'd worn before, she was certain—and a starched white shirt. Only his tie was a contradiction to his classic apparel. Today it was panda bears tumbling over themselves, munching bamboo. The black-and-white pandas and kelly-green bamboo looked absolutely ghastly with the navy suit. But rich boys, she supposed, could wear any ugly tie they pleased.

She stared out the windshield at the hazy morning scene of Alexandria-near-the-Potomac and wondered why she had agreed to let this spoiled brat pick her up this morning.

"So," she said as she adjusted her seat belt, "you're Marcus Masters the Third. Marcus Masters's kid."

"No. I *am* Mark Masters. The adult son of a man whose name is Marcus Masters, whose father also happens to be named Marcus Masters."

He was still smiling, but not quite so brightly now, and Kitt thought, *Touchy, touchy.* She wanted to say, No, you are the spoiled son of a man who doesn't care how he pollutes the culture as long as it makes a profit. But she steered clear of that honey pot. This was the congressman's new intern, and she couldn't do anything to jeopardize the CRM's position with Congressman Wilkens.

"Well, *Mr.* Masters—" she couldn't help the sarcasm "—exactly how did you happen to obtain this plum of an internship with Congressman Wilkens?"

"Don't call me Mr. Masters." The smile was gone and his face looked suddenly older, hardened. "That's my father. I'm Mark."

So this *is* some kind of sore point, his father. "Not Marcus?"

"That's my father as well. And Mac is my grand-father. I'm Mark."

"Does everybody call you that?"

"Only since I've been born." Now he smiled.

"Okay. *Mark.* How?"

"My father didn't pull strings for me if that's what you're asking. I applied for the internship like every-body else, and I got it."

"Yes," Kitt said, eyeing the supple leather up-holstery, the walnut trim, his handsome profile as he steered the car smoothly through the tangle of rush-hour traffic, "I imagine it was just that simple."

He cocked an eyebrow at her, a dark slash of dis-approval. "Rich does not equal spoiled."

She blushed at his perceptiveness, and he smiled, but not warmly. "I get this all the time, *Ms.* Ste-vens."

Kitt turned her face to the window. All this Mr. and Ms. doo-doo was purely antagonistic posturing, but even so, she did not invite him to call her Kitt. A tense silence ensued as they waited at one of the interminable stoplights that control the infamous five-way intersections in northern Virginia.

"So you study at the Carl Albert Center?" she said after a moment, trying to be civil.

"Yes, ma'am."

She ignored the ma'am. "Is that your major? Po-litical Science?"

"I study writing."

"Writing?" Kitt's own undergraduate major had been journalism, in its own way as tough a nut to crack as law school. "I'd think writing would be somewhat quaint and antiquated for the LinkServe genius."

"Do you actually know anything about my LinkServe experiment?"

"I know it's a comprehensive communications technology that you've been working on ever since you graduated from creating video games in high school. I know it's the technology that threatens to make other technologies obsolete. I know you—and your *father*—don't want LinkServe—and others like it—regulated by the new bill designed to control the glut of filth and violence in the media."

"I see I'm not the only one who does my homework."

"Is that what you call it? Homework?"

"Yeah. What do you call it?" He watched the stoplights above them.

"Espionage. Skulduggery."

He had glanced over then, blue eyes sparkling with challenge, and had given her a crooked little smile, which she had wanted to slap off his pretty-boy face. "You don't like me much," he said. "I can tell."

"I wouldn't say that I don't like you personally, Mark," she answered.

"Oh, what don't you like *impersonally,* then?"

Your father, the way he's polluting the mindscape of this country's kids for the bottom line, she thought. *The way he's planning to use LinkServe to keep on doing it, no matter what kinds of legislation my people get passed.* But, again, she avoided all that by squinting at his chest and saying, "It's your *tie* I think."

He laughed—a surprised, delighted laugh—and flapped the tie. "Hey. Don't knock it. This tie is a gift from a girl with impeccable taste."

"Oh, yeah?" Kitt imagined he probably had *girls with impeccable taste* buying him gifts every day of the week. And then, for some reason she couldn't fathom, she'd turned ten shades of red, and, trapped right there in his Lexus, all she could do was turn her face to the passenger window again.

Thank you, dear Congressman Wilkens, she'd seethed, *for arranging this delightful week with this delightful young man.*

WHEN KITT FINISHED her phone calls, she found him with his butt propped on a corner of one of the volunteer's desks, his handsome head cocked to one side, listening intently while two women and one man blasted their faces off with flushing zeal about the future plans of the Coalition for Responsible Media.

And in his palm he held a microrecorder.

"What's that for?" Kitt charged forward, pointing at the thing.

He stood. "I asked Mary and Shirley and Howard—" he smiled at the three "—if I could tape their comments. My memory is sort of feeble," he explained, then smiled again at the trio, who beamed back.

"But you didn't ask *me*," Kitt said. "Turn it off."

Mary's and Shirley's and Howard's smiles shriveled and they looked stunned, offended. At Kitt.

She ignored them. "If you want information, we'll get you some literature. Follow me." She whirled away.

Behind her, she heard him making his apologies to the group, saying maybe they could visit more later.

When she got him alone in her tiny office, she closed the door. "Don't do that again."

"Do what?" His face was guileless.

"Record the staff's comments. This is a coalition, and a very loose, diverse one at that. Made up of child advocacy groups, church groups, parents, cops, educators. Most of these folks are not political players. They're volunteers. They believe in what they are doing, but they are very naive. Did you even tell them you are an intern from Wilkens's office? That you're gathering data to report to the congressman?"

"Nobody asked."

Just as she'd thought. "Listen, Mr. Masters—"

"Mark," he corrected.

But at that she only squinted and repeated: "*Mr. Masters,* those folks wouldn't, of course, ask. They wouldn't know to ask. And while I appreciate your efforts to be accurate—"

"That's right. I'm only striving to be accurate." He raised his palms in a helpless gesture. "I have a very poor memory. In fact—" he pumped his eyebrows Groucho style "—I have absolutely no memory of the first three years of my life." He dropped his hands and grinned.

But his silly joke and his goofy grin did not amuse Kitt. "While I do want your report to the congressman to be as accurate as possible, you surely realize there *are* people who are anxious to undermine what we're doing here, to make us look like zealots, like twenty-first century thought police."

"How can I undermine you if I simply give the congressman the facts? You don't have anything to hide here, do you?" He smiled that smile. That smile that, Kitt was convinced by now, he surely must know was completely disarming and endearing. Completely sexy.

"From now on just stick with me," she said.

"Like ugly wallpaper." He pumped those eyebrows again, smiled that smile.

Kitt looked pointedly at his tie. He should know from ugly.

And the remainder of the day went like that: Kitt feeling threatened, edgy, thinking mean little thoughts; Masters being sunny, straightforward, thinking only heaven-knew-what. Smiling, smiling, smiling that damn winning smile. All the while Kitt felt certain he was gathering data that would somehow be used against her cause, given who he *really* was. Intern, schmintern.

He had to be doing everything he could to protect his LinkServe—how had he phrased it to Wilkens?— *his interests?* Interests indeed.

She felt despair when she realized that by some grotesque twist of fate, Marcus Masters's own son had become their unsympathetic pipeline to Congressman Wilkens. And The Pipeline seemed to be everywhere, getting into everything, persisting in being so *nice* that the staff was blinded to the dangers of opening up to him. Their underfunded little organization would be laid before the Masters Multimedia giant like a deer caught in the headlights of a semitruck.

By late afternoon Kitt was exhausted from the mental gymnastics, and the very sight of Mark Masters was giving her a torpid headache. She couldn't wait to get him out of their offices, to get away from the man.

But Jeff Smith neatly destroyed all hope of that when he arrived shortly after five to offer Kitt a ride home.

She went to gather her paraphernalia: jacket, clutch, pager, cell phone. While she crammed it all into her tote, Jeff reviewed their plans to go to Murphy's, her favorite Irish pub in Old Town. A little too loudly, Kitt realized, when she saw Mark Masters's head pop up from a stack of deadly-dull media-content analysis statistics.

"Hey! I've heard of that place!" Masters said from across the room.

Jeff turned. "Oh?"

"Yeah. One of the other interns mentioned it. Authentic Irish music, live." Masters smiled that choirboy smile. "Sounds neat."

Kitt wished to heaven the man would stop saying *neat*.

Mark's reminder that he was the congressman's intern was not lost on Jeff. "Would you care to join us?" said Jeff, the charming congressional aide, being hospitable to the lonesome little intern. "Whatdaya say, Kitt? Don't you think Mark should get a taste of authentic Alexandria nightlife?"

"Well..." Kitt knew she looked caught, trapped again, and she tried to compose her expression into one of nonchalance as Mark stood and crossed the room.

She shrugged. "Well, Murphy's isn't really a good example of Old Town nightlife. It's pretty dull, actually. The place would bore Mark, I'm afraid."

Mark gave her a small frown, cocked his head, regarded her with glittering eyes that seemed to see right through her. "I'm not nearly so prone to boredom as you seem to imagine," he said. "And how could anything be dull—" he paused, narrowing those already-narrow eyes at her "—as long as *you're* there."

Kitt's face flamed, and she opened her mouth to speak, but Jeff wedged his lanky frame between Kitt and Mark. "Does that mean you'll be joining us?" he asked.

Mark quirked a dark eyebrow at Jeff. "Absolutely. How do I get there?"

CHAPTER FIVE

THE PLANK DOORWAY to Murphy's Irish Tavern was so narrow that Mark actually had to tilt his shoulders sideways as he squeezed in. He stood inside a cramped little vestibule, allowing himself a moment to adjust to the dim lighting, the noise and the pressing crowd.

Mark hated crowds, and he was already thoroughly sick of the trendy Washington bar scene—self-important men in overpriced suits, narcissistic women in clever little day-to-evening getups. Tonight the regulars were doing their best to outshout each other over loud music in this dark forty-by-sixty room saturated with smoke, strong cooking odors and humidity that floated up from the Potomac like clingy polyester netting. Grateful that he'd left his jacket and tie in the Lexus, Mark rolled up his shirtsleeves and stepped into the melee.

A svelte woman said, "Excuse me," while brushing up against him as she passed. She made an elaborate business of raising two full glasses to shoulder level, to emphasize, he supposed, her trim shape, sheathed in a brown dress that poured over her curves like melted chocolate. The dense perfume she left in her wake clogged his sinuses.

Three girls, ponytails pulled through baseball caps and cleavage spilling out of athletic spandex, smiled from a nearby table and one raised a glass of ale at him. A woman at the bar turned her head, arched her back and lowered her eyelashes as he passed.

Mark spotted Kitt near the back of the narrow room. Squeezed into one of the old high-backed booths, with Jeff and that blond girl Mark had seen at the ice-cream social.

As he made his way to the booth, a trio onstage struck up a rowdy rendition of "Gary Owen," making normal conversation strenuous and even shouted greetings difficult to hear.

"Mark!" Jeff jumped up. "You found us!"

Mark tried to discreetly wipe the sweat from his temple. "This place is certainly tucked in here, like you said," he shouted at Jeff. "Had to circle the block twice before I found it, and a couple more times looking for a parking space." He glanced at Kitt. Although she smiled up at him, she looked as if she couldn't make out his words.

"Yeah, well," Jeff hollered in Mark's ear, "I guess Alexandria's a far cry from Oklahoma, where everything is surrounded by miles and miles of absolutely totally nothing.'' Jeff backed up a fraction, gave him a bland smile.

Even though Mark was not a native Oklahoman, he was irked by this condescending attitude. ''Not *absolutely* totally nothing.'' He smiled back, parroting Jeff's redundancy. ''There is the occasional Injun teepee.''

Jeff's smile frosted a bit.

Kitt still seemed unable to hear the men above the music, but her eyes narrowed as if she had become aware that something was subtly amiss. ''Mark—'' she leaned forward ''—this is Lauren Holmes, one of my roommates. Perhaps you two met at Congressman Wilkens's ice-cream social.''

Mark extended his hand to the blonde, and she offered hers with that fingertips-only handshake some women employ.

''Sit down!'' Jeff yelled and slapped Mark's back, pointing to the seat next to Lauren. Then he squeezed into the booth beside Kitt.

Were Kitt Stevens and Jeff Smith a couple? Mark studied Kitt. The moment he'd seen her at that ice-cream social, he'd thought, *Now there's an interesting woman.* Okay. More than interesting. Attractive. He'd found her even more intriguing at Gadsby's, and downright fascinating as he observed her in her offices today.

She glanced at him, brushed her bangs out of her

eyes self-consciously, and he realized he was staring. He turned his face toward the singers. Steady, boy, he told himself. Think of Tanni. Always of Tanni. Don't let yourself get all hot about a woman you don't even know.

"How about a beer?" Jeff, the grand host, offered.

"Have a Harp," Kitt shouted, "the best of Ireland." She raised her glass. The orange glow from the green-shaded lamp hanging over the table enriched the color of her hair to a honey gold.

Jeff jerked his thumb at Kitt's glass of Harp. "The only alcoholic thing she'll drink, but she claims Harp is some kind of patriotic ritual. Murphy's and church are about the extent of her social life, you know." Jeff winked at Mark and then grinned at Kitt indulgently.

Kitt smiled at Mark. An impudent little smile. "Irish music and a glass of Harp are good for the soul," she said, then closed her eyes and broke into a mellow, perfect-pitch harmony with the singers onstage. Some song about a minstrel boy.

Above her singing, Jeff teased, "Maybe good for the soul, but not the ears."

Without opening her eyes, Kitt jabbed Jeff in the ribs, and sang louder. Jeff clutched his side, feigning injury, then covered his ears.

Ignoring this silliness, Mark fixed his gaze on Kitt,

but spoke to Jeff. "Actually, she has a beautiful voice."

Abruptly, she opened her eyes and stopped singing. She blushed, he noted with satisfaction, most attractively.

"Please. Don't stop." He smiled.

She gave him a quick wide-eyed stare, then dragged her gaze to the singers onstage, and picked up the melody. But her singing was softer, more subdued now.

As the last strains of the music died away, Kitt looked into Mark's eyes. While they studied each other, a crease formed between her eyebrows, and her lips parted. Mark's gut tightened and a quickening shot to his groin as he watched her mouth.

The crowd was applauding and cheering, Jeff and Lauren with them. But Kitt and Mark continued to analyze each other in motionless silence.

The waitress came. Mark smiled up at her, then fixed his gaze back on Kitt and said, "I'll have a Harp, please." He glanced back up at the waitress and added, "And could you run me a tab?"

"Sure," the waitress said as she scribbled on her pad. But then she gave Mark a closer look and hesitated. "Uh, may I see your ID, sir?"

Mark leaned forward, extracted his billfold and flashed his driver's license.

"Thanks." The waitress gave him a second glance, smiled in apology and left.

"Bet you get sick of that," Jeff piped up. "How old are you, anyway? If you don't mind my asking."

"Twenty-seven," Mark said flatly. "And you?" He asked this with his eyebrows raised as if this were a real conversation and not a put-down contest. From the first, he'd suspected Jeff had some kind of territorial thing about Kitt.

The little blonde smiled into her beer glass.

"Old enough not to get carded," Jeff answered, and draped his arm on the booth behind Kitt.

"Congratulations," Mark said dryly.

This time it was the blonde who stepped in to calm the waters. "So, Mark, you're in Washington on an internship," she said.

He turned to Lauren. She was pretty, but not like Kitt. Not fascinating. "Yes," he answered. "And I'm also doing some stringing for the *Dallas Morning News*."

Kitt nearly lunged across the table, grabbing his wrist. "You're a *reporter*?" she said.

He looked at his wrist. She released it. "Not yet," he answered. "I'm only a cub. I don't really know what I'm doing. Yet."

"That's why you took this internship," Kitt said, realization dawning on her face. She made it sound like a crime or something. "And you're already stringing for the *Dallas Morning News*," she challenged. "*That's* what you were doing with that microrecorder."

"I was putting out feelers for a feature, that's all. Just an idea. They don't have to buy it."

Now Kitt's green eyes flashed like heat lightning. "Don't you have some ethical obligation to *tell* us that?" She was practically shouting. Mark noticed that people at surrounding tables were glancing their way.

"If I decide to actually write it, sure. But right now I'm just researching, seeing if there's a story there. You know, something along the lines of the tiny idealistic coalition taking on the media giants."

"Just researching? You were recording people's remarks." Now Kitt was shouting, and her face was getting redder by the second.

The duo onstage struck up a livelier song, a Scottish ditty about two young ladies peeking under the kilt of a passed-out drunken Scot.

Kitt pointed an accusing finger at Mark. "You were extracting material from sources who didn't know they were sources."

"Kitt, this is not a courtroom," Jeff tried to calm her.

"Oh shut up." She whirled her head at Jeff, and her hair made a glittering saffron fan over her cheek.

Mark pointed at the pint glass of Harp in front of her. "How many of those have you had?"

She spun her face back toward Mark. "I'm perfectly clear-headed." Kitt pounded the table with her fist. "What I want to know is what you were planning to do. Paint our organization as zealots—fools? Anything to undermine the CRM's efforts to limit the violence and filth glutting the media? Anything to help your daddy profit off his dirty rock-and-gangsta rap? Anything to clear the way for your precious LinkServe to operate free of constraints? Is that it?"

Mark eyed her. Even if she was a little stewed, it was obvious she meant every word. He matched her ardent fire with the cold sobriety of a stone. "No, ma'am. That is *not* it. I do not work for my father. And I wasn't being sneaky. I told your people I was recording them. And I haven't done a feature article yet that wasn't totally unbiased—"

"Unbiased? How can you even pretend to be unbiased about the CRM when you yourself are the developer of that…that LinkServe monstrosity?"

"Monstrosity? *Monstrosity?* This happens to be the twenty-first century. Technologies like LinkServe are here to stay."

"The CRM is only trying to protect children from undue violence and sexually explicit material. Seems to me that used to be a given in this country, before kids with guns and dirty music became common-place. No thanks to Masters Multimedia.''

''Masters Multimedia has nothing to do with guns, and as for dirty music, et cetera, we didn't exactly invent it.'' He cocked his head toward the stage, where the duo was still singing the bawdy Scottish song. ''Just listen.

''This nonsense has been around for ages. Think of all the old Scottish, Irish, Appalachian ballads that are full of murder and mayhem, not to mention—pardon my French—*sex.*''

Kitt glared at him, picked up her Harp, took a swig, then carefully lowered the glass to the table. ''Oh, this *nonsense*—'' she made quote marks in the air with her fingers ''—has been around all right, in the form of subtle innuendo. Like that last one. But not a dirty word in it. Even in the most tasteless old drinking songs, it's all innuendo. Nothing explicit. I have nothing against sex…or fun. But there is a vast difference between bawdy old tunes for adults and the stuff your father's company—'' she shook her finger at him—twice ''—*your* company, is produc-ing, packaging and distributing to children—''

His mouth opened as he tried to say something about it not being his company, or about First Amendment rights, or about parental responsibility, but Kitt charged on, shouting over the music.

''Stuff so violent—'' she actually jabbed his chest

this time "—that it's threatening to change the very fabric of this country. Kids *are* listening to those lyrics, they memorize them, they adopt their worldview. As the saying goes, it takes a village to raise a child, Mr. Masters, but today the village is destroying the child, all for the sake of money," the word *money* came out *muh-nee* and Mark recognized a trace of Okie accent. "The CRM's goal—and mine—is to halt that trend, Mr. Masters—" she jabbed again "—and neither you nor your rich daddy can stop us!"

The rich-daddy crack left Mark so blistered he was momentarily speechless.

Their eyes locked and it was as if Jeff and Lauren had shrunk to vanishing points at the edges of the room. And in that moment, Mark thought he felt something pass between himself and Kitt Stevens, something mystical but real. Her eyes, green as emeralds, were flashing, reflecting the fire in his own, he guessed.

He saw that she was looking at him, too, in a way no other woman ever had. Really looking at him. Into his eyes. And suddenly it hit him. This woman was the one. The One. Which was totally crazy. Surely he was imagining this, whatever it was. He tried to regain control. But it didn't work. He felt shaken. And again he thought, as plainly as if it were a neon sign flashing behind the bar: She's The One.

But The One broke off their eye contact, rummaged around wildly in her oversize tote and tossed a twenty on the table. "Let me out." She nudged Jeff out of the way. "I refuse to drink Harp with the devil."

"The devil?" Mark repeated sarcastically.

Kitt scooted to the edge of the seat, then twisted toward Mark before she stood up. "'Knocked yo' mama outta her bed,'" she rapped. "'Jumped her bones and split her head.'"

"Dead Tuna," Mark informed her. "Nobody takes them seriously."

"The hell they don't," Kitt retorted, and stood. "You should check your own company's sales records. Five hundred thousand copies sold and those precious lyrics inside every CD jacket." She hoisted her tote over her shoulder and whirled away before Mark could respond.

"Sweetie! How will you get home?" Jeff whined at her departing back.

"I'll be fine," Kitt retorted as she pushed through the crowd.

Jeff stared after her for some seconds, then resettled himself in the booth. "The lass has a bit of a temper on her, a bit of a temper," he said with a dreadful Irish brogue, which irked Mark at him afresh. What business did Jeff Smith have, apologizing for her? Jeff Smith wasn't responsible for Kitt Stevens.

But yes, Mark warned himself, his face still scalding from her verbal excoriation, the woman has apparently got a temper. And a fantastic mind. And a kind of righteousness that he found both intimidating and thrilling. A righteousness he envied.

He glanced at Lauren next to him. She smiled uncertainly, her face betraying acute embarrassment. Much as he wanted to leave, he'd stay long enough to smooth this over with her. After all, she wasn't to blame for the tremors rumbling beneath the surface between him and Kitt Stevens.

CHAPTER SIX

MARK ARRIVED at his apartment wondering why he'd done it. Taken the devil's—okay, *her* word—the devil's advocate stance once again. Defended his father's viewpoint. Spouted his father's rhetoric. Everyone already assumed he was some kind of clone of the old man. So why was he always doing dumb things that reinforced that notion?

He used his keys quietly, unlocking first the inter-grip rim lock, then the dead bolt, then the knob latch. Urban life in D.C., he thought morosely, inviting further self-doubts about why he had dragged his family up to this hellhole.

He slid the door shut, fastened all the locks and crammed his suit jacket and tie into the tiny closet off the narrow entry hall. His clothes were wedged in there like overstuffed files, but his daughter and his sister needed the larger bedroom closet.

He sighed. Small as it was, this walk-up was costing his father a fortune every month. But at least it was in a decent area—Alexandria—and being near the enormous First Baptist Church made Carly happy. She trooped over there every week, some-times twice, taking Tanni with her.

He slipped his shoes off to keep from making noise on the parquet floor and immediately stepped on something sharp.

He stooped to pick it up. One of Tanni's fashion dolls, half-dressed, the bleached-blond hair matted like a Brillo pad. The neglected condition of the doll bothered him but, he reasoned, isn't this the way most four-year-olds treat their toys? Still, he made a mental note to speak to Carly about teaching Tanni to take care of her things.

He glanced at the plastic mounds of the doll's bosom in the semidarkness and remembered Kitt Stevens's remark about the village destroying the child. Maybe the woman had a point when a thing like this was considered appropriate for a little girl. What could Tanni possibly be learning by toting this crea-ture around? That to be a woman she needed pencil-thin legs, an eighteen-inch waist and a giant bust?

He tossed the doll on the hall table and went into the living room. Carly was asleep on the couch, her fair skin and long dark hair contrasting eerily in the glare of the TV. He frowned. Perhaps he was ex-pecting too much of a nineteen-year-old, even an enormously self-assured one like Carly. He'd let her take on the responsibility of being a mother to her niece—his daughter. How long could this whole setup last? What about Carly's plans for her life? Her education? He would simply have to double his classload after he finished this internship. Then he'd find a job and get his sister back on track.

Of course, Carly missed their mom, too, but she said she was okay, as long as they were all together. At least that's what she kept telling him. He looked down at her and grinned. She was sleeping with a Bible pressed open across her ribs. She'd been reading her verses but—he glanced at the TV screen where David Letterman was making cracks—she'd also stayed up to catch the Top Ten.

He left the TV on for the moment and went into the bedroom to check on Tanni. She was sprawled on the queen-size bed, a tiny princess floating in a swirling sea of sheets. Muggy air flowed in from the open window beside the bed. Another thing he would have to speak to Carly about—leaving windows open at night in the heart of Alexandria, even if they were up on the third floor.

He walked quietly to the bedside and looked down at his daughter, love bursting in his heart. She had gone to sleep without seeing her daddy this evening. He hated that. No more stupid evenings in trendy bars, he vowed. *Even if you know Kitt Stevens will be there?* he countered himself. Yes. Even then. No more late nights.

He knelt by the bed, smoothed the frizzy tendrils

of dark hair from her warm forehead. She made a little sucking motion with her mouth. He smiled. Not so long since her binky days. His smile widened when he recalled how he had worried about her refusal to give up that pacifier. Because she didn't have a mother? Had been deprived of breast-feeding, not to mention so many other things, tangible and intangible? And then one day she tossed the pacifier out the window of the Lexus as they were flying down the interstate. "Bye, bye, binky!" she'd called cheerily.

He studied her tenderly, vowing again to spend more time with her. After all, wasn't that what he wanted? The reason he'd paid Tiffany to go through with the pregnancy?

He stood and gently scooped her into his arms, carried her into the bathroom and sat her down to tinkle—she was so proud every time she made it through the night dry—and the whole time she never even opened her eyes. After he tucked her back in the bed, he tried to lower the window soundlessly, but it was old and made a terrible racket. Tanni didn't stir, but from the living room, he heard Carly's sleepy voice, "Mark? That you?" Good to know that at least she would wake up if there was a disturbance.

He went back to the living room. "Yeah, I'm home. How'd it go today?" He crossed to the thermostat and turned it down, then flopped into the sagging easy chair opposite the couch.

Carly swung her legs over the side of the couch. Laid her Bible on the coffee table, yawned and stretched. She stared at the TV screen for a second, picked up the remote and said, "Hush up, fool," to Letterman as she clicked it off. "It was a good day. We walked to the park. Had spaghetti, watched *Full House* reruns. Not bad."

"I'm sorry about taking the Lexus, Carly. But I can't expect this lawyer lady to ride around on the back of a Kawasaki ZX–11."

"Why don't you ever just call that thing a motorcycle?"

"Because you don't call the fastest, sleekest, meanest machine in the known universe a moe-tore-sigh-cull." He started to unbutton his shirt.

Carly shrugged. "I don't get it. Why do you have to give this lady a ride? Surely a lawyer has her own car."

He couldn't answer that. Why did he? "It's only for this week," he evaded.

"So, are you picking her up again tomorrow?"

It occurred to him then that he and Kitt had not made those arrangements. But the way she'd stormed out of Murphy's, he assumed Kitt Stevens would rather hop to work on one foot than accept a ride with the "devil."

"As it turns out, I guess I could take the Kawasaki tomorrow, and you and Tanni could go to see some sights. But be careful driving in this Washington traffic. Don't go out before ten in the morning—"

"—and come back here before four to avoid the rush hour," she finished for him. "You are talking to a woman—" Carly always referred to herself as a woman since her momentous eighteenth birthday a year ago "—who has driven on the Santa Monica Freeway at five-fifteen, for crying out loud. All I want to do is take Tanni over to see those friends of Daddy's in Fairfax. Speaking of Daddy, he called."

Mark finished unbuttoning his shirt. Here it comes, he thought, long-distance micromanagement. "What'd he want?"

"To know if we had enough money, of course. He also thinks you need to let Felix make you at least one more suit." She frowned at him. "He's right, you know."

He made a snotty-sibling face at her. It wasn't bad enough that she'd taken over the apartment and the food and Tanni, now his little sister was fussing over his wardrobe. Someday, she was going to make some poor guy mighty miserable. "The suit I have is fine. I also have a sports coat and two perfectly good pairs of slacks. Besides, where would I hang more clothes?"

"In a bigger apartment, if you'd let Daddy spring for it."

"Look, Carly, we agreed on all of this before we came out here. I know it's not what you're used to back in sunny old Carmel, but if you want to stay with me this summer, if you want to get away from Dad—" he spread his arms "—this is it. This is my life. Besides, I owe Dad enough money already."

Carly stretched. "I told Daddy you'd just spend the money on clothes for Tanni anyway. So he's sending it to me." She grinned. "I'll know what to do with it."

Mark rolled his eyes. Then he pointed at her. "You'll waste it all on that church."

"It's not wasting, you bum, it's tithing. You should try it—and a lot of other things while you're at it." She raised her nose in the air and fiddled with the delicate cross hanging from a sterling-silver chain at her neck.

Mark rubbed his forehead. This was not what he wanted to do: endure a late-night sermon from his sister. His head was droning with all he'd seen and heard at the CRM today. He needed to open his laptop and make notes. "Time for bed, Carly."

"Somebody else called. A woman named Trisha Pounds." She picked up a slip of paper off the coffee table and held it toward him.

He didn't take it.

"Who is she?" Carly studied the name.

"Dad's idea of someone I should get to know."

"Should you?"

"Doubt it."

"Hey." Carly frowned at the slip of paper. "Is this Trisha Pounds, the weekend anchor on *Washington At Nine?*"

"The same." He massaged his neck.

"Man! She's a real knockout!"

"A knockout media personality wouldn't necessarily make a stable mother for Tanni."

"You shouldn't be thinking about that when you date people."

"The hell I shouldn't."

"You should be thinking about what you want."

"I've already done my fair share of thinking about myself, thank you. Would you just can the advice for the lovelorn tonight?"

"My, aren't we crabby!" Carly tossed the phone message down. "Did you eat any supper? There's some spaghetti left. I've got some romaine for a salad, too, and I could throw in a nice glass of carrot juice." Carly was unwavering in her convictions, a devout born-again Christian and a Southern California animal-rights vegetarian. These things Mark tolerated—even if his father didn't—because he loved her.

Mark smiled benevolently at his sister. "Yum. Romaine and carrot juice. All I've had is a nasty old Harp and a stick of beef jerky.''

"Gross. What's a Harp?''

"Irish beer. Positively poisonous.''

"Alcohol and petrified animal flesh. Some supper. And besides, drinking's a sin,'' Carly said over her shoulder as she headed to the kitchen to warm up the spaghetti.

"I try to offend in every way that I can,'' he hollered after her. He threw his head against the back of the saggy chair and smiled. Carly. So much like Mom, worrying about his clothes and his nutrition. His smile dissolved. *Don't think about Mom,* he commanded himself. Don't think about what a mess your life has become since she died. Not tonight. Think about the future. Only the future. The future you are building for Tanni.

But he did think about his mother, later, after he'd eaten Carly's pasty vegetarian spaghetti, after he'd typed his notes into the laptop, after he'd checked on Tanni one last time. When all the lights were out, when he lay on the couch-made-bed, as he listened to the noises of the traffic outside the stuffy little apartment, he thought about his mother. From the beginning, his mother had been the one who'd wanted Tanni, fought for her. Her stubborn love had given Mark the chance to fall in love with his own child, had given his father the grandchild he adored.

He thought of his mom's promise that she would always be there for Tanni. How could she have known that breast cancer would nullify that promise?

Of all his mother's qualities, it was her voice he remembered the most vividly. He'd sometimes imagined he'd heard echoes of her calling out his name in the huge Spanish-style house in Carmel, long after she had died. He remembered the sound of her— talking, laughing, singing.

Out of the blue his next thought was of Kitt Stevens, singing that Irish ballad. He could hear her ugly parting shot, too, the obscene lyrics by Dead Tuna about killing a mother. Of course, she had no way of knowing his own mother had been dead less than a year. Or did she? From what he could gather, she did her research as thoroughly as he did his. And suddenly, Mark felt annoyed at Kitt Stevens.

In the next instant he felt old, much older than his twenty-seven years. And tired. And alone. Mostly, he felt so very alone.

He flipped onto his stomach, punched the pillow into submission and tried again to sleep. Though Carly provided fresh sheets, the couch beneath them smelled musty and stale, the Washington air felt sticky and thick, and the lights from the street pierced like lasers through cracks in the drapes.

He kicked a leg out from under the sheet, letting his foot flop to the floor. He always slept in boxers and kept a sheet over himself in case Tanni or Carly came in, needing him in the night. Normally he didn't mind, but tonight the coverings felt as heavy as chain mail.

He flipped onto his back, pushed the sheet to his waist, folded his arms across his broad chest, closed his eyes and exhaled a frustrated sigh. *Sleep,* he ordered his body. *Tomorrow is another wonderful, hectic day in our nation's capital.*

But his body did not want to sleep. His body, it turned out, wanted Kitt Stevens.

CHAPTER SEVEN

KITT TOOK a long sip of steaming herbal tea—the only thing her stomach could tolerate—and allowed herself a moment of reflection before plowing into the day's work. She gazed out her narrow office window to the tree-lined street below. The morning sun etched long shadows up the sidewalks, and between profiles of buildings, she could see the river in the distance, where a thick summer haze indicated that the day was developing into a scorcher.

She'd gratefully accepted when Jeff offered her a ride this morning. She supposed he assumed that she would not be riding to work with their charming Guest-of-the-Week, Mark Masters.

Ride-sharing had solved that perennial Old Town problem, parking. But the real problem this morning was what to do with Mark Masters. She took a sip of tea, considering.

Jeff had offered to keep Masters busy in the congressman's office over at the Rayburn Building, and though Kitt longed to be relieved of the obligation to entertain the intern, she declined.

Masters would take his removal to the Rayburn for what it was: chickening out, both professionally and maybe—she tried to deny it, but couldn't—personally. And it might piss off the congressman. She took another sip of tea, tried to calm the butterflies in her stomach. She frowned at her reflection in the glass. Thought about last night.

The trouble was simply that Masters was so good-looking. He resembled Danny. That's all. Elemental chemistry. She had forsworn any involvement with that kind of man. Too much pain. Abruptly, she again saw the scene that had haunted her for the past four years. The cheerless green walls. The stirrups. The nurse's sympathetic eyes.

The baby's tiny face.

To blot out that memory, she concentrated on the present, on the activity in the street below.

Her eye was drawn to a man on the opposite corner, dressed incongruously in a motorcycle helmet and dark business suit, parking a purplish-black monster motorcycle. Her brothers had owned motorcycles in college and Kitt smiled when she imagined the boys' reaction to a sleek piece of equipment like that.

But what kind of man would drive such an in-your-face racing machine in downtown Alexandria? It wasn't as if they were in Oklahoma or Texas where corners were few and far between. He had to be a little…odd. Intrigued, she continued to watch.

The man removed his helmet. Mark Masters! He balanced the helmet on the seat, ran his hands through his thick hair and gave his lapels a jerk. The butterflies in her stomach fluttered wildly.

She checked her watch. Seven-forty. Good Lord. What an overeager beaver. She watched him as he extracted a slim satchel from the pannier case.

His every move exuded pure athletic grace. Man, did he have the physique. She didn't know if her cheeks felt suddenly hot from noting that or from the sudden photo-flash memory of their encounter last night. Lord! She'd made a perfect ass of herself. She'd even cussed, if she remembered right. When would she break that revolting habit, the legacy of four older brothers? Damn, damn and double damn!

In turn, Masters had been all cool reasonableness, even if he was ethically, morally, legally wrong. Hair-splitting self-justifier. Rationalizer.

But she worried. How did *he* see *her* now? Now that she'd flashed her famous temper? How was she ever going to face him this morning?

He was watching traffic, waiting to cross the street, and suddenly, he looked up to the third-story window where she stood, *looked right at her,* with those eyebrows slanted together in that sharp vee that made him look so...so...Lord, she didn't *know* what, but it wasn't good. She wondered if the morning sun was reflecting off the window. She hoped so. She backed up a fraction. Then she changed her mind and stepped forward, raised her mug in greeting. He gave her a pithy little salute. She raised her chin.

But as he crossed the street, she felt a surge of panic. They would be alone up here, at least until the volunteers started arriving at eight. Oh God.

She dashed into the cramped bathroom off her office. She checked herself in the mirror. Too pale. The freckles on her nose stood out like tattoos. She muttered, ''Woman, you don't look so good,'' to her reflection, then dumped the tea down the tiny sink, brushed her hair wildly and touched up her lipstick. She ran out, unlocked the front office door, returned quickly to her office and composed herself in her desk chair. She heard him taking the stairs two at a time and grabbed a document, pretending to peruse it just as he rapped on her open door.

''Good morning!'' he called out cheerfully.

Oh, this was going to be a fun one, this long, hot day in the perpetual company of Mr. Mark Masters.

''May I come in?'' he asked, smiling.

''Uh. Sure.'' With a concerned frown, she ''read'' the document, seeing nothing, then looked up. ''Uh. Would you like some tea, or coffee, or something?''

''No thanks. Are we alone? There are a couple of things I want to discuss with you.'' He stepped up to her desk, holding the helmet casually against one hip, with the attaché case dangling from the other hand.

"Yes, I believe we're alone." She laid the document aside. He eyed it, frowning as he read the title upside down. Only then did she realize exactly what she had been fake-reading. Someone had clipped an interview of a raunchy rock band from *Playboy,* complete with the full-color pictures on the back side. That's the visual he'd gotten when he walked through the door: the top half of a *Playboy* centerfold. She felt herself turning positively purple. She reached to turn the offending document facedown, then realized this would only leave the nude shining up between them. She folded her hands primly over it.

He raised one eyebrow.

"Research," Kitt said, businesslike. "Yes. We're alone. What did you want to discuss?"

"First of all, I would have picked you up today, but I didn't think you'd want me to." His face was a portrait of sincerity. "So I just came in on my bike. I guess I got through the traffic a lot faster that way." He raised the hand holding the briefcase and looked at his watch. "Wow. Seven forty-five. Anyway, after last night—"

"Don't worry about it. I have a Jeep, Mi—" She stopped herself before the haughty-sounding "Mr. Masters" slipped out. She fixed her eyes on his stupid tie—parakeets this time—vowing to control herself. But her face felt like a broiled tomato.

He spoke calmly. "Well, I just wanted you to know I didn't forget about you or anything. No hard feelings about last night." He put the satchel on the floor and extended his hand—that tanned, very muscular male hand—over her desk.

When she took it, he held her fingertips, and her gaze, as he said, "You know, I'm not exactly Filthy McNasty." She tried to pull her hand free, but he held it, gently but firmly. "And I'm not the devil, either. I'm just a guy who's here to learn." His hand was warm, steady, powerful. His eyes were sensitive, serious, sincere.

She withdrew her hand, shoved her bangs aside, and stammered, "I...I...no hard feelings at all. You are entitled to your opinion. I just happen to think you're wrong." She shuffled papers on her desk. "Perhaps you only need more facts. Perhaps we can remedy that while you're with us here at the CRM."

He shrugged. "Maybe. But my job is to get information for the congressman. Not for myself. Actually, I agree with you about some of that stuff, but, hey, kill the messenger. Masters Multimedia just manufactures entertainment. We're not the artists who create it. We're not the consumers who buy it."

"But you do profit from it. You make it accessible. And the distinction is moot when we're talking about children's minds.'' Kitt rose from her desk and crossed the room to a computer monitor tucked in the corner. ''There are some things on our Web site that might help you with your report,'' she said as she switched on the machine. ''Use any of this information you like.''

She leaned down, keeping her eyes on the screen, clicking the mouse as she brought up the site, hearing him cross the room behind her.

He stood close. It was amazing how she could feel him: his bulk, his heat, his breath. It was amazing how good he smelled. *Stop it, Kitt.* Didn't you learn a thing from the Danny episode of your life?

''The distinction is relevant,'' he said as if she'd not changed the subject to the Web site. ''Last night I was wondering, besides the fact that you hate us for being Masters Multimedia, what do you really know about my family?''

She turned and faced him even though she knew her cheeks must be as red as sin. ''I don't hate you for being Masters Multimedia,'' she said. ''I *oppose* you. And as for what I know about your family, the answer is…not much. I mean, after all, I didn't even know you're a reporter.''

''I'm a *student* of journalism,'' he corrected.

''A student who's already stringing for the *Dallas Morning News,*'' she corrected.

He put his palms up. ''Okay, okay. That's not

what I'm talking about. I asked, what do you know about my family?''

''I know you sell a lot of hideous trash you call entertainment, and because of that you're wealthy. And I know you're about to get a lot wealthier, as soon as you can get every household in the U.S. dependent upon your precious all-encompassing LinkServe.'' Kitt pushed her bangs aside self-consciously. She couldn't imagine where he was going with these questions, but she didn't have anything to lose. Certainly not after last night. ''I know you'd like to knock this pesky regulatory legislation out of your way.''

He made a dismissive face, shook his head impatiently. ''You don't understand. LinkServe technology will make the legislation obsolete before Congress even passes it. And any entertainment Masters Multimedia is forced to abandon here will simply pop up from a foreign market. Government regulation isn't the answer.''

She started to counter that, but she couldn't because he had just neatly summed up her two biggest worries.

He shook his head again. ''I'm not talking about politics anyway. I mean, what do you know about us personally? About my parents. My father? My mother?''

''Not much. Really.'' She thought she saw an immediate softening, a kind of relief, spread over his face that she didn't understand. "In fact," she added for emphasis, "I know so little that I thought *you* were your father at that ice-cream social."

"You thought I was my *dad?*" he said. Then he gave her an amused, disbelieving frown, and added, "And yet you rebuffed me so cruelly?"

Kitt had to grin—and blush—at the memory. "No! When I did that I thought you were just another conceited guy. Later I thought you were your father. And then I found out who you really were even later, at Gadsby's."

She watched as realization dawned on his face, and then he laughed. And laughed. He laughed so hard he ended up holding his sides and gasping.

"What's so funny?" she said, feeling a little piqued as he convulsed with laughter and pointed at her.

Between gasps he explained, "It's just that *I* was feeling asinine because—" he caught his breath "—because I'd had the stupidity to hit on my dad's number-one opponent, of all people. Ms. Katherine Stevens of the Coalition for Responsible Media. The name and the title sounded like she'd be some—" he sputtered "—shriveled-up old crone."

Kitt couldn't help laughing. When she got her breath, she said, "You were pretty cool about it. I thought you knew who I was all along. When did you figure it out?''

He waved his fingers up around his head. "It was the way you kept fiddling with those braids, like they really bugged you, and I thought, Wait a minute, she's the blonde from the reception. And then I thought, Uh-oh, Kitt is short for Katherine." He broke up again. "Oh man," he said, wiping at his eyes. "And then I knew something else was wrong. The way you and Jeff Smith both looked like you'd been stabbed or something."

Kitt pointed at him, nodding and giggling. "I'll just bet we did!" Then she added, "And then the…the congressman—"

"—stuck us here together!" he finished for her.

They both broke up again, and Kitt lightly punched his biceps the way she did with her brothers, then she grabbed his arm to steady herself as her giddiness weakened her.

He stopped laughing, looked down at his arm, then at her face. The look in his eyes halted her laughter in one breath. She dropped her hand.

He started to say something, leaned toward her, but she turned away and grabbed the mouse again. "Well," she said, "that's what bad poop'll do for you in this town. Jeff's the dodo who told me you were Marcus Masters, meaning your father." She wondered if she sounded as shaky as she felt. She shouldn't have touched him! She fixed her eyes on the screen, shaking her head, trying to appear nonchalant. "But I knew something didn't add up. I figured you looked too young to be the real Marcus Masters."

She had located the Web site, and, managing a valiant smile, whirled to tell him this. His face was only inches from her own, and deadly serious. "I *am* the real Marcus Masters," he said. "I told you, I just happen to have the Roman numeral three after my name."

She frowned. It was as if all the levity had suddenly been sucked from the room.

"Are you planning on using me to get to my father?" he said.

Kitt held her breath. "What?" she said in a horrified whisper.

"You heard me." He pressed closer.

"Of course not," Kitt protested. His face was so close she could feel his breathing. She tried to turn away, but he blocked her, trapped her in the corner of the computer table.

"You wouldn't be the first. In fact, it cuts both ways. My father was ecstatic when he heard I got this internship. I figure he only wanted to use me to influence the congressman. Are you trying to use me, too?" He pinned her with his burning blue gaze.

Kitt felt herself blushing again—she didn't know

if it was because of their proximity or because what he said was partly true. She *had* wanted to influence his father, had wanted to convince him the media bill was necessary and inevitable. Had she wanted to use Mark to get to his father, or at least to solidify her position with Congressman Wilkens? "There's a lot at stake with this bill, a lot you don't understand," she said.

"I know more than you think. That isn't what I asked you." He stood his ground. "Were you planning to use me?"

Kitt squeezed her eyes shut and shook her head. "I would never use anyone. *Use* is the wrong word. I want to…" She faltered as she looked into his eyes. "I want to educate, to sensitize you. You *and* your father."

"Then educate me, sensitize me," he challenged, leaning forward slightly.

Their breaths mingled. And for that millisecond, as he kept his eyes, so blue, so serious, fixed on hers, she was afraid he might actually kiss her or something. *Stop it, Kitt! Do not get involved with this man!*

She averted her eyes, breaking the spell. "All right," she said breathlessly. "We can start with the Web site, and there are links, of course." She twisted her torso and fumbled to her side for the steno chair that had been bumping her thigh. "H-here," she stammered. "You can use this chair." She put a palm up as if to press his chest away, and he stared down at it, then backed up.

"Thanks," he said, and started removing his jacket. Eye level with his chest, Kitt couldn't help noticing the well-defined muscles bulging under his shirt.

She darted around him to the safety of her desk.

"Is it always this hot in here?" he asked as he peeled off the jacket and settled in the steno chair.

She eyed his back, huge above the dinky back of the secretary-size chair. *Only when you're near,* she thought. "It can get pretty muggy," she answered, and wondered how she was going to get anything done with that massive back in view all day.

"PRETTY MUGGY" didn't even come close to describing the office a few hours later, when the sun reached mid-sky and the wheezing old window-unit air conditioner exhaled a death rattle.

All the volunteers were fanning themselves, sipping ice water, complaining, and Kitt had already made three very assertive calls to the landlord, who insisted on sending his own maintenance people out to do the repairs "as soon as humanly possible," which, Kitt knew, could mean sometime next November.

Working on an empty stomach in the heat soon gave Kitt a throbbing headache.

But Mark Masters remained annoyingly cheerful. He persevered at the cramped computer station the entire morning, carefully copying data—with Kitt's permission—onto a floppy disk he'd taken from his satchel. Sometimes he whistled. Sometimes he turned and flashed a companionable smile at Kitt, who tried to keep her mind on her endless stream of phone calls, on making arrangements for the upcoming Parents for Decency rally in July.

The parakeet tie had been jerked off and discarded on a nearby table. Watching him loosen it, Kitt had felt a sensation low in her abdomen that she refused to identify.

Suddenly he jumped up and crossed the room, carrying the yellow legal pad on which he'd been scribbling notes.

"Your Web site's pretty good—run by volunteers, huh?"

"Yes. Our main problem is money, not manpower."

He smiled as he came toward her. "Have you got time to answer a couple of questions?"

"Sure." Kitt laid aside her day planner and tilted her head to concentrate on the pad he held in front of her.

"This Dave Lambert, he's the anticensorship activist, right?" Mark tapped the name.

"Yes," Kitt acknowledged.

He leaned closer, pointing at another line on the legal pad. He smelled wonderful! And this close, she could again feel heat radiating from him, she even felt his hot breath when he spoke. "And on this date, Lambert was responding to the American Medical Association's condemnation of raunchy rap lyrics last summer?"

"Yes." She swallowed. Was she salivating because she'd skipped breakfast?

"Interesting." He smiled.

She looked up into his eyes, trying to read what he meant by *interesting*. But of course, those eyes were unreadable, so deep-set, backlit by the window behind him. His face was softly flushed—from the heat?—and the hair around his forehead was damp. The shadow of his beard was coming in, though it wasn't even lunchtime yet.

Kitt's phone buzzed and they both jumped like teenagers caught doing something indecent.

She snatched up the receiver as if this were a call from the White House. "Yes?" she breathed. "Oh. Hi, Jeff. Hi."

Mark straightened and moved to the opposite side of the desk, where he could collect himself. Because the fragrance of her hair, the color of her eyes, had almost undone him. And what he'd seen when he glanced down her V-necked camisole, he definitely shouldn't have seen that—for his own sake. Pearls draped on creamy skin, flowing over two perfect, delicate mounds.

The way she blushed was so appealing. She was doing it now.

"No, no. I'm not too busy, just answering some of the intern's questions—"

The intern?

She laughed then, no doubt at some crack the witty Jeff Smith had made.

Mark didn't like the sound of it.

"That sounds great," she said. "I'm starving and I'm dying to get out of here. Our air-conditioning is broken again... Oh, Jeff, you're so sweet."

Oh, Jeff, you're so sweet. Why did everything about Jeff Smith bug the bejesus out of him?

"I'll ask him." She covered the mouthpiece, looked up at Mark. "Jeff wants to know if you want to go to lunch with some of us. We're just going someplace nearby."

Mark considered. Tanni and Carly were out in Fairfax visiting his dad's friends. No need to run home to check on them, as he'd frequently done since coming to Washington. "As long as it's air-conditioned," he said.

"Jeff? He says yes.... Lauren?" She gave Mark a

glance. "Sure. Bring Lauren.... Okay. We'll meet you downstairs. Okay. Bye."

Kitt hung up the phone, looked at Mark again. What was his problem? Why'd he look so...bothered all of a sudden? It made her nervous. *He* made her nervous. "Jeff was on his cell phone," she explained. "With Eric—not on the phone with Eric—I mean, in his car—I mean on the phone in his car—with Eric." She was babbling. "They're only a block away. Come on." She jumped up and grabbed her jacket, then tossed it aside. "I've got to get out of here," she jabbered on. "I feel like a stewed tomato." She bit her lip. Poor choice of words! Her *brain* must be stewed.

He was smiling. An indulgent, polite, but slightly smirky smile. No doubt remembering their conversation about sexual innuendo last night.

KITT'S STEWED-TOMATO face fell in dismay when she got downstairs because Jeff and Eric pulled up not in Jeff's spacious, cool-cool-cool-air-conditioned Lincoln Mark VIII, but in Eric Davis's cramped little LeBaron convertible. The one on which the top stayed down from March until October, come wind, frost, or as today, hellacious heat. When they parked at the curb, Jeff hopped out and said, "I'll ride in back with the girls."

"I don't mind the back," Mark said, then got in,

and held the bucket seat forward while Kitt climbed in. Jeff folded himself in right beside her. Lauren shrugged and smiled at the Eric guy then took the front seat.

Kitt, crammed between two sweaty males, seemed instantly testy. "Why on earth did you guys bring this car, today of all days?"

"Eric wanted to bring it," Jeff inclined his head meaningfully toward the blond in the front seat.

There was no place for Mark to comfortably rest his arm but across the back of the seat, behind Kitt's head.

Evidently picking up on Kitt's ire, Jeff started chattering like a nervous talk-show host.

"Okay, folks, this *is* a little cozy but, in any case, we shouldn't have far to go." Eric pulled into the tangle of traffic. "Fortunately, there are a zillion great places to eat in Old Town. What'll it be?" No one answered Jeff. "So, how do we all feel about La Madeleine's?"

Silence.

"Something to please every palate there."

Still no response from the audience.

"What do we say, La Madeleine's?" the host pressed.

"You like French country cuisine?" Eric asked, leaning toward Lauren.

She nodded as she pointlessly fiddled with the air-conditioning controls.

"Fine," Eric said to Jeff.

"To La Madeleine's," Jeff smiled and made a flourish with his hand. The talk-show host keeping things moving, keeping things lively.

Mark wished Jeff *could* keep them moving. They were stuck in a crawling train of cars on a narrow side street with the sun bearing down overhead. He felt as though his face was frying. He studied Kitt out of the corner of his eye. The ovals of pink on her cheeks that had looked so attractive earlier had developed into angry crimson splotches.

"So, no A.C. at the old office?" Jeff started up again. "Tough day for it." He leaned forward and addressed Mark, "Hottest summer I've ever seen in D.C. And I've seen some scorchers." Jeff leaned back and spoke toward Kitt's hair, "But the heat certainly hasn't taken the bloom off you, my sweets. You look as fresh as a flower today."

Mark glanced down at Kitt. The flower was definitely wilting. In fact, she had an awfully disgusted look on her face and her lips were pinched together so tight they had turned white. Mark prayed this restaurant wasn't far, willed the damn red light to change and tried his best not to sweat.

"'Course, people don't realize the D.C. area can get as miserably hot as it does," Jeff continued, leaning forward. "It's because of the humidity. Washington is built on a wedge of swampland between two rivers."

Now it's a travel show, Mark thought.

"So it's your basic urban hell, and you see tourists all the time, wilted, waiting in an endless line in the broiling sun to get into the Washington Monument, which is nothing but a giant oven—" Smith's nattering felt, in the white-hot Egyptian heat, like a woodpecker drilling a hole into Mark's forehead.

Kitt's soft groan below his shoulder made him turn just as he felt her head bump heavily against his arm.

"—and the constant road construction, stalling traffic like this—" Smith was saying.

"She's fainted!" Mark shouted. "Kitt! Kitt!" He brought his arm down and pulled her to him, bumping Smith, who was saying "What the—"

"Get this damn car out of the sun!" Mark bellowed at Eric, who looked back wildly, shifted gears, gunned the engine and roared backward, almost hitting another car.

"Kitt!" Lauren called out, trying to reach into the back seat and fan Kitt's face.

But Kitt was totally unconscious. Her lips looked white, her skin felt clammy. Eric blew the horn and cursed, but couldn't extract the car from traffic.

Mark said, "Move!" and jabbed Jeff. "I'm getting her into the shade."

"I'll take her." Jeff rallied and tried to take hold of Kitt, but Mark pinned him back against the seat. "Just move it!"

"Kitt, wake up!" Lauren pleaded.

Jeff managed to stand in the seat, and hurled his lanky frame over the side of the convertible. He attempted to tug Kitt's shoulders from Mark's arms. "Let me have her!" Jeff demanded.

Mark hooked one arm under Kitt's knees and hoisted her onto his lap. She seemed to be waking up as her head lolled against his shoulder. Mark focused on getting Kitt out of that baking back seat. "You carry her legs," he said to Jeff.

Lauren had jumped out of her seat to hold the door open and the bucket seat forward. Jeff took Kitt under the knees, succeeding in ripping a hole in her panty hose with his watch as he lowered her feet to the pavement.

Mark said, "Hold her up," as he folded her shoulders forward and jumped out of the car.

Kitt started to moan, and as he jogged around the car, Mark looked for someplace cool to take her. "In there." He indicated an optician's shop.

He shoved Smith aside and pulled Kitt forward by the arms, but Jeff was not to be dismissed so lightly. He tugged on her shoulders. When they tried to stand her up, Kitt's legs buckled like soda straws, and the men ended up with her sagging between them, elbows cocked skyward. Passersby stared.

"Let go of me," Kitt mumbled as her head lolled weakly.

"Yes, let *go*," Mark said angrily as he struggled to lift Kitt into his arms.

"*You* let go," Jeff countered, not releasing his hold, and complicating Mark's task.

Mark groaned as he scooped her up. He staggered across the sidewalk, and while Lauren held the door, he carried Kitt into the shop. Jeff scooted in alongside, uselessly supporting Kitt's body with his palms.

As soon as they hit the cool air of the shop, Kitt came fully awake. "Put me down," she said firmly.

The woman in the shop rushed from behind the counter. "Is something wrong?" she asked. "Should I call 911?"

"Yes!" Mark and Jeff said in unison.

"No!" Kitt protested, and struggled against Mark's chest. "I'm...I'm all right. For heaven's sake, *put me down*." She tugged at her skirt.

He lowered her feet to the floor, but did not take his hands off her, holding one palm against her ribs and one against her back as he studied her face.

Smith kept his hands on her, too. "What happened, sweetie?"

Swaying, Kitt shoved at both men's chests, but neither released his hold. "I think my blood sugar's low," she said, rubbing her forehead, "and I...I just got too hot, and then everything went black."

"Could we please get some water?" Mark asked the shopkeeper.

"Yes, some water," Jeff echoed.

Mark guided Kitt to one of the vinyl waiting chairs, seated her, knelt on one knee before her.

The shopkeeper bustled back with a paper cup of water and Jeff grabbed it and brought it to Kitt's lips. Mark tried to take control, sloshing the water down Kitt's front. Jeff tried to brush off her chest and Kitt slapped his hand away.

The shop lady ran back in with a damp paper towel for Kitt's face, and the same childish struggle was repeated as the two men tore the towel in half. The lady frowned. Kitt frowned. "Would you two stop it! I just need to eat something."

"Can you make it down to Trattoria Dio, sweetie?" Jeff patted her hand, "It's close by."

Kitt nodded.

"One of us better go out and find Eric and Lauren and tell them where we're going," Jeff said, effectively dismissing Mark. "Trattoria Dio. Right around the corner. Eric knows where."

Mark turned to go. He had no idea where Trattoria Dio was, so he couldn't take Kitt there himself. Jeff Smith had won this round, he realized. And as soon as he had that thought, he wondered when the hell it had become a competition.

AT THE RESTAURANT Kitt remained irritable while Jeff ordered for her and called her "sweetie" enough times to ruin Mark's appetite. He ordered only a cold pasta salad, as did Lauren and Eric.

Mark assumed that Jeff imagined he was speaking perfect Italian when he ordered, "al pollo a calamiori" for himself and Kitt.

What was that? Mark thought. *Pig Italian?* He assumed Jeff meant el pollo carciofi, but instead the fool had ordered something with squid.

The waiter, snide and sweaty from the lunch-hour rush, didn't bother to clarify. He cocked an eyebrow and wrote on his pad, then snapped up the menus.

"The air-conditioning in here ain't makin' it," Jeff announced. "Let's douse this." He blew at the candle, causing the flame to shoot sideways and set the paper napkin in the bread basket on fire.

Lauren yelped.

Mark tossed his water on it.

Kitt rubbed her forehead.

After a little stir, the waiter materialized like a punitive fire marshal and relocated them to an undersize table where nearby smokers made breathing seem like a bad decision.

The food arrived, and Kitt took one look at the

huge serving of chicken swimming in sauce and squid, excused herself, and bolted to the ladies' room. When she didn't return after a lengthy time, Lauren went to check on her.

The men finished eating in a deafening silence, and mercifully, the check came. Jeff plucked it up between thumb and forefinger. "Allow me to buy your lunch."

Mark ground his teeth. He couldn't afford to pay the check in a place like this, but all the same, he was sick of Jeff Smith's Big Daddy act. But sparring with this fruitcake was ridiculous. "Thank you," he said.

For she was what he wanted. When had he realized that?

No matter. He knew it now, and it was time to do something about it. Because he also knew that if you never run the play, you never make the touchdown. It was time for a long pass, so to speak. He grinned at his own pun. If Kitt weren't acting so cantankerous right now, he might share it with her. Have a laugh. He remembered her face as she'd excused herself from the table. Better not.

Jeff paid and the men made small talk, waiting on the women, who seemed to have taken up residence in the ladies' room. "Maybe we should go get the car," Eric suggested.

Jeff and Eric walked down a curving iron staircase

and then out the door. They hadn't noticed Mark hanging back.

To kill time, he picked up some mints, then stopped outside to wait for Kitt and Lauren on the canopied patio by the sidewalk.

He propped a foot up on the long bench that hugged one wall and considered what to say: *Are you and Jeff Smith an item?* No. Way too forward. And if she said yes, that would be the end of that—no chance to plead his case. *Which is what?* he wondered. He couldn't come out and say, *I am incredibly attracted to you and this happens to me about as often as a solar eclipse. In fact, the last time I was this attracted to a woman, I got a child out of the deal, who is now a feisty four-year-old.* That would send her running. He'd sound like some kind of undersexed Vulcan, and the fact that he was a single dad would probably scare the pee out of a high-powered female attorney on her way to the top. He could say something like, *I'd like see you alone.* Oh, right. Then he'd sound like some kind of stalker. He rubbed his forehead. He was overthinking this.

When the women finally appeared on the patio, he still had no idea what to say and simply blurted, "We need to talk," as he stepped into their path.

"Oh, hi, Mark," Lauren said.

Kitt fixed him with the kind of suspicious look one

would give a deranged person on the Metro, and he thought, *Relax. She thinks you're weird.*

"I...I mean—" he ran a hand through his hair, quickly clamped the hand back down to his side "—I mean, are you okay?"

Kitt nodded warily.

"She just needed to wash her face," Lauren volunteered.

"That's good. Kitt, I really need to talk to you...about...about something." He smiled at Lauren apologetically. "Alone."

"I'll go catch up with the guys." Lauren ducked around him and was gone.

Kitt gave him a skeptical frown. "So. Talk."

"Not here. This is serious. I need to meet you someplace...someplace away from...away from everybody at the CRM and away from...from everybody connected with Wilkens's office." He didn't know where the hell that had come from. Jeff Smith, he supposed. Why was he being so weird about this? Couldn't he just say he wanted to get to know her better? But twice now she'd dodged him. And without sufficient motivation, he was afraid she'd do it again.

"This has something to do with the congressman?" Now she looked alarmed, but intrigued, definitely intrigued.

Okay. Maybe he would just play it that way, and

come clean later, when he had her alone. "Well, not the congressman, exactly," he said confidentially. "His *people*. Look, is there someplace where we can meet and talk privately, without anyone else around?"

"His people? Does this affect the CRM?"

"Uh. It could. Look. We can meet anywhere you choose. In the daytime. In a public place, as long as no one will be able to hear us."

She studied him, weighing this. "Okay," she conceded. "Somewhere public, yet private?" Her eyes brightened and she snapped her fingers. "Dumbarton Oaks. It's a public garden surrounding an old mansion, the kind of place where we could see people coming, and even if someone should recognize us, it's frequented by tourists, and we could say I was just showing it to you." He was pleased to see that she was apparently getting into this cloak-and-dagger routine.

"Dumbarton Oaks?" he said.

"You can't miss it. Ten acres at the corner of Thirty-second and R Streets. But it's only open afternoon hours." She looked at her watch, chewed her lip, flipped those bangs back, and he thought, *Adorable*. "Can you be there around three o'clock?" She looked up at him, "They close the gates at six. Is that enough time?"

Enough time? Three hours? She was going to give

him three hours out of her hectic day? In a garden? Though he was not religious, Mark wanted to fall on his knees in gratitude.

But he kept the grin he felt bubbling up firmly off his face and with a grave nod said, "I suppose I can go anytime I want. I'm still working in your office."

"Oh. Right. But we can't leave there together. The volunteers are so nosy. I'll leave early, get our tickets, leave yours at the gate. There's a little guardhouse there—they'll give you a map—and I'll meet you inside the grounds at the pool house. It'll be cooler there and I'll be concealed while I wait for you."

"Okay," he said. "The pool house." He was tempted to add, *Should I say something like, "Mary had a little lamb," when I walk up?* But he wasn't about to give even the slightest clue that this whole thing was a farce.

"Well, I suppose the others are waiting," she said.

"Yes." He kept his expression serious—the expression of a gentleman burdened with heavy secrets. He indicated the lady should precede him down the patio steps, and as he walked behind her, admiring that mane of reddish-gold hair, he wondered what in the hell he'd done.

But then he thought, at least you're in the game, buddy. At least she had agreed to talk to him. Alone. It's a first down, man. You don't have to know every detail of every play at this point.

CHAPTER EIGHT

DUMBARTON OAKS LOOKED like one of those gardens from an ancient, much more romantic, time. As Mark walked through the ornate wrought-iron gates, instead of immediately worrying about what he was going to say to Kitt, all he could think was what a perfect setting this was for their first time alone together.

The grounds were dominated, of course, by towering oak trees, but also there were many other varieties that Mark couldn't identify. Gnarly old things, with as many roots exposed as they had primeval limbs dipping to earth. As his shoes crunched on gravel paths dappled with sunlight, he marveled at the lush beauty around him.

Worn brick paths set in patterns of diamonds and ovals wound among hedges and lawns clipped as precisely as carpet. Everywhere he looked, stones were set in extraordinary patterns, sculptured topiaries grew like alien life-forms, and flowers, flowers, and more flowers, spilled over in the hot sun.

He heard fountains splashing in cool counterpoint

to the sultry air and farther off, birds called out from high in the trees, sounding wild and exotic.

Out on the street it was unmercifully hot, but in here, among so much foliage, with the fountains ionizing the air, it wasn't half-bad, and for that, Mark was grateful. The trip over from Alexandria to Georgetown on the motorcycle had done nothing to enhance his appearance. He imagined that the sweaty thatch on top of his head was way beyond help and he could feel giant semicircles of perspiration forming at his armpits.

This meeting was a crazy idea and about to get a whole lot crazier.

With the aid of the map he'd received at the guardhouse, he found the pool house easily. She was there, as she had promised, sitting back under the arched spaces, in a wrought-iron patio chair, against a wall covered in a mosaic of fleshy Grecian nudes that contrasted with her slim power-suited elegance. She stood when she saw him approaching. She had removed her jacket, and he tried to keep his eyes off her thin camisole, which, in the humidity of the garden, outlined her curves as clearly as those of the Greeks on the wall behind her. He worried. What to say? How to begin?

"Hi," he said. God, she looks so beautiful, he thought, as if she had just stepped off the pages of a catalogue.

"Hi," she said. "Did you have any trouble finding it?"

"Not really," he lied, then corrected himself. "Well, actually, I took a wrong turn, ended up crossing Memorial Bridge, crossed back on Roosevelt Bridge, went through some place called Rosslyn, crossed Key Bridge. I done seen my share of bridges, ma'am."

In fact, his frenzied drive over from Alexandria had been like some pathetic docucomedy: *A Fool's Guide to Washington's Bridges*. With each wrong turn, he had panicked, fearing that she would leave before he found the place. He tried to unobtrusively wipe the sweat from his forehead.

"Pierre L'Enfant is immortal, all right," he continued, referring to the French architect who'd designed Washington. "Thousands of tourists curse his name every day." He smiled.

She did not smile back. "There's a spot that might be a little cooler and more private down below. Follow me."

Kitt headed down a corridor of high hedges interspersed with banks of nodding daylilies.

She went to an ancient-looking concrete bench, set deep in the shadows of an enclosure that was as dark and archaic looking as a Roman tomb. It was a level below the pool, hidden by archways and tangled grapevines, looking out over some real vegetable gardens, which were wilting in the afternoon sun. But surprisingly, a breeze stirred in this grotto, carrying with it the rich scent of garden soil and the distinctive aroma of the colonial boxwood. Only the sound of water dripping somewhere broke the silence.

She lowered herself onto the bench and indicated he should do the same.

Mark sat, put his helmet on the ground, squirmed a second and said, "I hope you're okay, being out in the heat and all. After fainting earlier, and all." Geez. He sounded like an absolute churl. His head pounded and his heart drummed. What to say? What to say? He hadn't pursued a woman in so long.

"I'm fine. Lauren brought me a frozen yogurt at the office. It's pleasant down here, don't you think?"

"Yeah. This place is really neat. I love plants and flowers and stuff, you know."

"Really?"

"Yeah." Mark made a swipe at his hair, attempting to tame it. "I think they're neat." *Oh boy, Masters. Another minute of your wit and she's going to just jump right into your arms.*

She filled his uncomfortable pause. "Well, we didn't come here to discuss the gardens. What is it you want to tell me?"

His stomach tightened. He looked at her and thought, *I want to tell you that you are The One. That we belong together.* But what he said was,

"Well, it's...uh...it's complicated. But first I want to apologize for coming on so strong in your office this morning. I don't always think so clearly when it comes to my father and Masters Multimedia, although I try. I really do." He gave her an apologetic grimace.

"Look," Kitt said, "I understand. We got off to a bad start, I think."

He felt a surge of hope.

"I'm edgy about this media bill," she went on. "So much is riding on it. There are times when working for the CRM is extremely taxing."

She looked so small and fragile when she admitted that, that he wanted to wrap his arms around her. To kiss her. "I know what you mean," he said. "Working in this town can be overwhelming. Right now I just want to be a good reporter, the best reporter I can be, and my own man."

"I hope you know I wasn't planning on using you to get to your father," Kitt started to explain.

"Look. To be honest, there's stuff between me and my father that has nothing to do with Masters Multimedia. Just try to remember that I'm not my father. I don't even agree with him half the time. Okay?"

"Okay." Kitt smiled. She understood, better than he knew. Sadly, she was nothing like her mother, either. "Now what was it you wanted to tell me?" she said.

"Well, actually, it's about…before I get into it, I need to know, are you and Jeff Smith dating?"

"Dating?" She looked puzzled. "No."

No? While his heart did a merry little dance, he fumbled for a way to go on.

"No? But you *are* close friends?"

She still looked perplexed, but answered, "Yes. Occasionally we go out on what I call companionship dates, and Jeff's been very helpful to me since I came to Washington." She was frowning at him. "Now, what is it you want to tell me?" she insisted.

"Well…uh…then are you dating *anyone* from Wilkens's office?"

"*Dating* anyone? No." She looked downright confounded, and who could blame her?

Cut to the chase, Masters. "Well, what I mean is, are you dating anyone at all?"

"*What?*" she said, plainly incredulous.

"Because the thing is, if you're not involved with anyone, I'd like to date you."

"*Date* me?" She looked as if she failed to comprehend the meaning of the word.

"Yeah. You know. Real dates. Movies. Dinners. Walks at Dumbarton Oaks." He fanned an arm out toward the gardens.

She blinked repeatedly, as if she'd just been given a fatal diagnosis or something.

"You know," he fumbled, "have fun. You know, as in—"

"What?" she repeated.

"—go out," he finished lamely.

"Mark, do you know how *old* I am?"

"No. And I don't care."

She tapped her chest, as if he were some thick-skulled juror who needed dramatic gestures to hold his attention.

"I am twenty-eight years old," she said with deliberate slowness.

"Woohoo. Ancient." He found he was suddenly giddy now that he had put his cards on the table—however absurdly—now that it appeared she was going to actually argue the merits of this dating thing.

"I am older than you are." She was still speaking to him slowly and deliberately.

"Correct. I'm twenty-seven," he said.

"How come you're still in college?"

He was used to this. "I got a late start. Very late. Rich-daddy syndrome. You know. I partied and played around with the LinkServe model." He made a wry face at his own pampered past. "But one fine day I got...motivated. When I finish this internship, I've only got one year left. And besides, what has age got to do with it?" He went back to the original subject. "Do you want to date me or not?"

Somehow, that hadn't come out right, and he scrambled to say it better. "I mean, I'm sincere. You're...you're beautiful to me." That didn't come out right either. It sounded as if he was implying she was only beautiful *to him*, not, in fact, beautiful period.

Struck mute by his own stupidity, he grabbed her hand and fiercely, hotly, not at all suavely, kissed it.

She looked appalled. Her jaw dropped, her cheeks flushed and for a second she seemed in shock, oblivious to the tendrils of hair blowing about her mouth.

Then she snatched her hand away and closed her mouth in a hard line, said, "Absolutely not," and turned her face away from him.

He moved closer to her on the bench, leaning forward, trying to make eye contact. "You don't mean that. This is dumb, I know, the way I'm presenting it, but the other night, at Murphy's, you can't tell me you didn't feel...something—" She looked at him then. "I'm incredibly attracted to you," he said. She looked away again and folded her arms tightly around her middle.

"I am," he said. She looked back at him. "Tell me you don't feel the same."

She unfolded her arms and ran one hand through her bangs. "You don't even know me," she protested. "You're still calling me Ms. Stevens, for crying out loud."

"That's the idea behind dating, to get to know each other. So, what do you say? One little date? One drink? I could call you Kitt, and I'd let you call me Mr. Masters." He grinned but again she didn't smile at his humor. He continued, switching back to earnestness. "I'm only being so blunt because we don't have much time. I'll only be in D.C. for eight weeks. Don't you think when two people feel this much attraction they should pursue it?"

Kitt froze inside. Up until this point this little melodrama had been incredible, weird, but somehow honest, even charming. She might have eventually softened to his wacky charm, but that last speech sounded vaguely like Danny. *Let's have fun while we can and not consider the consequences.* Her instincts not to get involved closed around her like armor. "There are other things," she said, "other responsibilities to consider in a relationship besides those of the two parties involved. Dating is a serious matter with me."

"Okay, then we'll call them serious dates." He was only aiming to lighten the mood but she jumped up, and was out of the shadows and stomping up the winding stone steps before he could even mutter, "Damn," as he punched his thigh.

ON THE LONG WALK back to the Kawasaki, Mark pondered what he had done wrong.

Everything. Just everything. You don't initiate a relationship with a sophisticated, successful woman by blurting out Me Want To Date and slobbering all over her hand.

But throughout these recriminations, he held on to one tiny thread of hope: she wasn't dating anyone, at least not seriously. If she were, she would have offered that as an excuse immediately and ended the little scene.

He threw his leg over the Kawasaki, started the engine and gunned it with too much gusto. Two older ladies passing on the otherwise quiet sidewalk gave him censoring looks. He strapped on his helmet and flashed them a broad benevolent grin then lowered the face shield. How about that? Kitt Stevens wasn't dating anyone. Definitely a first down.

CHAPTER NINE

THAT ONE THOUGHT—Kitt Stevens isn't dating anyone—sustained Mark through the remainder of the week. While he worked steadily on his report for Congressman Wilkens and slowly gathered facts for his feature article in the *Dallas Morning News,* he plotted how to get Kitt to go out with him.

Kitt was working feverishly on some event called the Rally for Common Decency, which was scheduled to coincide with the big July Fourth celebration at the Capitol Mall. And she was carefully avoiding him.

She had all but punted him to the three volunteers, who, while very obliging, didn't know squat about the legislation, media research or much of anything else.

He also noticed that there were no more invitations to after-hours socializing *or* to lunch, and that Jeff Smith seemed to be finding a reason to hang around the CRM office every day.

Then, on Friday, his last day at the CRM, he saw his chance. Everyone but the two of them had left the office early. Kitt was still entangled in last-chance-before-the-weekend phone tag at her desk.

He tapped on her door and opened it a crack. She looked irritated, but signaled him to enter. He slipped inside, and stood waiting, as if he had some urgent business with her.

When she hung up the phone, he said, "I just want to thank you for giving me this opportunity to work closely with the CRM. My report to the congressman will be, I think, unbiased and thorough." He held out the papers.

"I appreciate that," Kitt said as she rose. She took the pages and leafed through them. Then she looked him in the eye and extended her hand formally. "Thank you for your time and consideration. I hope we've convinced you that the CRM's position on this issue is valid."

He took her hand, squeezed it. "I learned a lot here." He didn't release her hand.

She broke eye contact, tried to pull away, but he held fast.

"Could we start over?" he said quietly.

She removed her hand, folded her arms across her middle. "If you are going to bring up that dating thing again, it's…it's out of the question," she said.

"Why? Because you think I'm too young for you?"

She exhaled a long sigh. "No. *No,*" she said.

"That's not it at all. There's only a year's difference in our ages."

"Then what is it?"

Yes, Kitt, then what is it? she thought. But she knew what it was, exactly. And she knew she could never explain that to any man. "I just can't get involved with anyone right now," she said.

"I'm not talking about getting involved. Look, if we can't actually date, fine. But can't we at least be friends?" He smiled that smile, and looking at him, Kitt had to admit she liked him more than any man she'd met in a very long time. He certainly wasn't the kind of man you could easily dismiss. And he was only going to be in Washington as long as his internship lasted. There was no risk in being friends.

"Okay," she said. "Friends."

"Friends," he said. This time he offered his hand. When she took it he gave hers a quick, friendly squeeze and let go. Careful. He was going to be so careful with her this time. "Let's start by going somewhere just to talk," he suggested.

Kitt considered. One thing he certainly could do was talk. Mark Masters never seemed to be at a loss for words...or ideas. Except for the confrontation at Murphy's, she had genuinely enjoyed their snatches of conversation. "Okay. Where do you want to go?"

He spread his hands as if it was obvious and smiled. "Dumbarton Oaks."

THEY WERE MEETING much later in the day this time, nearer to closing time, and Mark had a plan. If he played his cards right, she would go to dinner with him when the gardens closed.

This time they met at the gate. And again she looked so beautiful that he felt a little short of breath when he spoke. "You changed clothes," he announced, as if she might not realize she had. She was wearing a peach-colored dress made of a filmy fabric sprinkled with little flowers.

"Yeah," she said, and fluffed the long, full skirt. "It's too hot for a suit and hose out here." She wiggled her toes, which peeked out of strappy little sandals.

But it was, in fact, not so hot this evening as it had been on their first visit, and the gardens seemed, to Mark, even more magical than before.

They walked.

Through an orangery where a fig, planted before the Civil War, hugged walls and beams. Past wooden benches, ornate wrought-iron gates and scrollwork, down the winding brick paths.

They talked.

She told him about the history of the mansion and the gardens. She named the flowering plants that intrigued him, identified the various trees.

He told her about how he got into journalism,

about the inception of the LinkServe model, about his treasured Kawasaki ZX–11.

When they came to a tiny balcony overlooking a pebble garden, Kitt read aloud the inscription set in the stone below a symbolic wheat sheaf: *Quod Severis Metes.*

"As you sow, so shall you reap," Mark said over her shoulder.

She turned, pushed her bangs aside, looked up at him with a bit of surprise. "Yes, that was the motto of the Bliss family who lived here. How'd you know what that meant?" she asked.

"Everybody knows Galatians 6:7," he said.

She smiled, truly charmed. "But does everybody know it in Latin?"

He tapped his temple. "Ed-jew-cay-shun, ma'am."

Kitt laughed lightly, and he adored the sound of it, did everything but stand on his head in the fountains to elicit it again and again.

At last they strolled a shady brick path called Melisande's Allee and ended up in a low area identified as Lover's Lane Pool; an oval stone pool set in a miniature Roman-style amphitheater, its mirrored surface serenely reflecting the towering English beech and silver maple trees encircling it.

Here the air felt cooler, damper, more secluded. The long evening shadows, the whispering breezes in the trees, the honey bees flitting among tall purple blossoms, created an atmosphere redolent with peace and privacy.

Here, Mark thought, he should make his move and ask her to dinner.

"Isn't this gorgeous?" she said effusively, spreading her arms, looking too beautiful, too fair, for words.

"Let me kiss you," he said quietly from behind her.

It wasn't what he'd planned to say.

She turned to face him, her mouth open in surprise.

"Just one test kiss," he said, and swooped down on her lips like one of the bees on a flower. Gently. Drinking.

She started to step back, but he crushed her body to his—the way he'd wanted to ever since he'd held her when she fainted—and immediately the kiss became more insistent, more sexual, and then completely wild, utterly passionate. Who was he kidding? This was no test kiss. This was The Kiss.

She whispered, "All right," against his lips when he allowed her to breathe, "maybe we could date…some…just to see what happens—"

"Good," he said and covered her mouth with his again, kissing her longer, harder. Finally he raised his head, looked in her eyes, and breathed, "Let's see what happens."

CHAPTER TEN

FROM THE START their dates revolved around those kisses that communicated everything, those looks that promised all. In those first weeks, it didn't matter where they were or what they were doing, Mark found a way to kiss Kitt.

They started out meeting for lunch every day, sometimes eating, sometimes strolling hand in hand on Alexandria's waterfront, sometimes meeting near Congressman Wilkens's office and ducking into cool corners in the huge Smithsonian museums on the Mall to talk...and to steal kisses. Sometimes they both took the Metro and met at Dupont Circle or Metro Center or Union Station, rode up the giant escalators, grabbed a quick bite to eat, browsed in bookstores, found quiet places to talk...and to kiss again.

After only a week of this, Mark was ready for more than kisses. But he kept his feelings in check, sensing that, with this woman, one false move might end it. She seemed like a delicate butterfly, ready to flutter out of his reach if he pushed for intimacy too fast.

And after only a week of dates, he started to won-der—to worry—if he should tell her about Tanni. He'd always sworn he wouldn't introduce Tanni to any woman until he was sure of the relationship him-self. But he was becoming sure of this thing with Kitt awfully fast, too fast. Some instinct—or was it just plain old fear?—warned him to take it slower.

Because he refused to accept any money from his father beyond the basic expenses for Tanni and Carly, Mark found himself chronically short of funds. This had not bothered him before he met Kitt, but now he was regretting his decision to live the pared-down existence of a struggling student. He wanted to take Kitt to nice places, surprise her with little gifts, send her flowers.

But Kitt didn't seem to notice his limited budget. She produced tickets to a Kennedy Center play for their first big Saturday-night date, and they both seemed content to do things that didn't cost much.

He persuaded her to ride on the back of his mo-torcycle, wearing his helmet. They took a spin along Canal Drive in her Jeep Cherokee. They rode the Metro together, talking and touching, while the train, sounding like a perpetual howling wind, roared through tunnels and over bridges, racing along a track of inevitability…like their relationship.

One evening they returned to Murphy's, this time alone. She laughed and called "The Rising of the Moon" "their song." And this time while she sang along with "Minstrel Boy," he pushed her bangs out of her eyes for her, and kissed her hands when she was done.

And then *she* kissed *his* hands, gently and comfortingly, when he told her about his mother's death.

"We still miss her. I guess we always will." He smiled sadly as if remembering something endearing. "Mom was so good with people, especially with—" He stopped, looked away, bit his lip, nodded slightly.

Kitt gave him his moment.

"Her name was Carolyn," he finally said, looking down into his Harp. "I can see now that she was the force holding our family together. I'm afraid the worst side of Dad has emerged since she died—his controlling side."

"His controlling side?" Kitt encouraged. She hoped she wasn't prying, but she couldn't help herself. She wanted to know everything about Mark Masters. Everything.

"Yeah. Controlling. As in, 'I have the money, and I call the shots.' He's so bad that he's driven my nineteen-year-old sister away. She should be in college, but Dad insists on telling her where to go and what to major in, so she's rebelling against the whole idea now."

"So, what is your sister doing with herself?"

Mark wasn't ready to reveal the peculiar details of his unconventional family situation, but even so, he refused to lie. He fashioned a half truth. "She's hanging out, best I can tell, doing a little child care." He smiled. "She's a good kid who just needs time to find herself."

"And what about you? Is that what you're doing in Washington? Finding yourself? Avoiding your wealthy, controlling father?"

Mark gave her a wry smile. "I've already found myself, thank you. As for avoiding my father, I suppose I am. His latest means of control is LinkServe. The long and short of it is, he'll fund LinkServe, but only if it means he can own me with it."

Kitt sighed, understanding completely. "I had a friend with a father like that once, back in Cherokee. A rancher. Offered to give her and her husband a huge parcel of land. He even offered to build them a house on it. Trouble is, it was right next door to *him*—the old man."

"Did she take the land?"

"No. She told her dad that she and her husband would accept the land, but that they were going to sell it and use the money to build their house in town."

"What'd the old man do?"

"What do you think he did?"

"Yeah." Mark leaned back in the booth with a sour look on his face. "Exactly what my old man would do. No more land. Right?"

Kitt suddenly wished she hadn't told the story. It had the wrong ending. She could see how torn Mark was. He was being forced to choose between LinkServe, his dream project, and his freedom. "This must be terrible for you," was all she could offer for comfort.

"Yeah. I keep hoping he'll calm down, see my viewpoint, but without Mom..." He sighed. "At least Mom could get him to see other people's point of view once in a while." He leaned forward and looked down at his hands, folded loosely around the glass.

"I'm sorry," Kitt said, gazing at the top of his beautiful head, and knowing that she was falling deeply in love.

He continued to stare into the ale, as if in a trance, and she wondered what he was thinking. She took one of his hands and kissed his knuckles lightly, letting her lips rest there for a moment.

With his free hand he brushed her bangs back again, then cupped her head with his large palm and laced his fingers in her hair. "You are really so very, very beautiful," he said quietly.

Never had Kitt gazed into eyes so sincere, so loving. How long, she wondered, could she resist those eyes? How long before their delicious kisses evolved into something they might both regret?

But there was no way she could deny herself the pleasure of just being with him. They could talk endlessly, it seemed. They talked so much that Mark started referring to their relationship as "our conversation."

And on every date, it seemed they found out things about each other that were surprising, things that were, to each of them, exciting and stirring. Each new fact seemed to fit in a pattern, to fuel hope, to foster dreams. Mark attended journalism school at the University of Oklahoma, and—guess what?—he *loved* Oklahoma; Kitt had grown up in Oklahoma, surrounded by four brothers, and—guess what?—she *loved* men. *Ha, ha.*

Kitt told him she had an old horse, Beetie, back in Cherokee; Mark told her he had several in California, but none that were named after a vegetable. *Ha, ha.*

"I was the victim of a traditional parochial Catholic education," Kitt pointed out one day as they watched a busload of uniformed grade-schoolers unload in front of the White House.

"Oh yeah?" Mark responded. "You don't know anything about being a victim until you've been the victim of several top-notch prep schools."

Then she told him what it was like to wear a faded

secondhand uniform year after year, and he told her what it was like to be picked up from football practice in a limo by your father's driver instead of your father.

He told her why he had chosen O.U. "To fit in. To be a regular guy for once."

She told him why she had moved to D.C. "To stand out. To be special for once."

The third week, they both played hooky from their offices one afternoon and met at Dumbarton Oaks again.

"Okay," he said as he pulled her to a secluded bench sheltered beneath the arms of an ancient Japanese maple, "let's get the kissing business over with."

Kitt punched his shoulder.

"You know you aren't going to give me any peace until we do," he said, and pulled her down on his lap.

"Oh, stop it!" she said, and struggled against his chest. She started to giggle but he gripped the back of her neck and took command of her mouth. Her giggles dissolved into moans.

He put one hand on her jaw, with his elbow pressed gently into her breast, and circled her hips with his other arm, drawing her closer to him. Kitt felt the magic he worked with his mouth from the top of her head to the tips of her toes. She actually felt light-headed.

She broke away, breathless. "Mark, this is shameless," she said. "Someone will come along and see us."

He splayed his hands around her ribs and bounced her on his knee as if she were a little girl. "Then I say we go somewhere where no one can see us." He pumped his eyebrows in that Groucho way of his.

Now Kitt's blush was genuine. "I'm...I'm not ready for that. I'm...I'm," she stammered, no longer sure what she was.

"You are the most beautiful, frustrating woman I've ever met!" Mark secured her in his arms and stood. "That's what you are." He pressed her against him and whirled her.

She threw her arms around his neck, and hung on tight, thinking that Mark Masters was the most adorable, magnificent man she'd ever met. Just for this one instant in time she wanted to stay in his arms, and think of nothing but him. As he spun her round and round Kitt laughed, and didn't care who saw them.

For his part, Mark could not make her laugh enough. Could not touch her enough. Could not taste her enough. And every night, every single night, after he'd chatted with Carly and tucked in Tanni, Mark fell asleep on his couch-made-bed with the same three thoughts: Kitt, Kitt, and Kitt.

Kitt now found his teasing use of the word *neat* endearing, especially when he whispered it against her neck after one of his glorious kisses. She was so giddy, so high, about this gorgeous, amazingly self-confident man pursuing her, now with open abandon, that before long, she completely lost sight of her old vow never to fall in love again. And every night when she tried to practice her old ritual of praying as she drifted to sleep, other, more earthy thoughts preceded her dreams.

But the dreams themselves seemed troubled. Not troubled in the way of the old nightmare; she was too happy, too distracted, for that, but troubled in a new way. These dreams nibbled at her like fish under a murky pond.

For even as they opened up to each other, even as trust flowed between them, even as their joyous in-fatuation blinded them, there seemed to be a kind of hangover the next day, the feeling that they'd gone too far, or…not far enough. For both.

Mark felt guilty about keeping his daughter a se-cret, despite his old vow never to expose Tanni to a string of women. Tanni had been so confused and forlorn after Carolyn's death. Mark was determined that his daughter would never suffer a separation like that again. Not if he could help it. He knew he should tell Kitt about Tanni soon, but a woman like Kitt would surely want to meet his little girl right away. No, he decided, it was easier not to tell her at all.

One afternoon when they were grabbing a hot dog on the Mall and watching kids crawl all over the statue of Uncle Beazley the dinosaur, Kitt had delighted in the youngsters' antics so much that Mark could tell she genuinely liked children. He had to literally bite his tongue to keep from repeating the latest cute thing Tanni had said.

Another time when they were in the East Wing of the National Gallery of Art, a preschool class toddled by, holding on to a looped rope with a teacher at each end.

"Forced march," Mark quipped.

Kitt's responding giggle made him forget himself. "When my daugh—" He stopped short.

"What'd you say?" Kitt said absently as she smiled at the kids.

"I said, cute, aren't they?" Mark evaded.

Kitt sighed, watching as a teacher herded the last of the toddlers around a corner like ducklings. "Yeah. Do you ever want to have kids?"

"Do I ever? I love kids."

I'll tell her about Tanni, he thought, as soon as I get to know her better. Or rather, after she gets to know *me* better; for Mark thought he already knew everything he needed to know about Kitt Stevens, that he loved her fiercely, and probably always would.

And, for Kitt, there was the one thing. Just that one thing, so long ago. *Eventually I'll have to tell him,* she thought as she watched the toddlers disappear, *if our relationship is going to be completely open.* Mark will understand, she assured herself.

It wasn't long before they gave up trying to keep their relationship secret, and after a few weeks, Kitt brought him home to meet her other roommate, Paige Phillips. Lauren had already figured the whole thing out in one glance one day after Mark had dropped Kitt off at the CRM offices following one of their long lunches. When Lauren commented again that Mark was just about the dreamiest guy she'd ever seen, Kitt's face had gone all rosy. "Kitt!" Lauren had breathed. "Are you and Mark seeing each other? *Dating?*"

"That's what he keeps calling it," Kitt had said, blushing higher.

"Oh my gosh." Lauren clamped her hands over her mouth in glee. "Our Kitt has a boyfriend!"

Kitt felt happier than she had ever been. Her energy level skyrocketed and she didn't even mind when Lauren asked her to take over teaching songs to the Sunday-school classes at the First Baptist Church.

"I HAVE SOME PEOPLE for you to meet, too," Mark told Kitt one evening as they cuddled by candlelight on her couch. "They're…very special. I was thinking we could all go out together soon, so you could get acquainted."

"I'd love to meet your friends," Kitt said, and gave him a happy squeeze.

Mark didn't disabuse her of the "friends" notion. Because he'd waited uncomfortably long to mention his daughter, he wanted Kitt to meet Tanni, to see her in person, before any complicated explanations were made. The fact that he had fathered a daughter, and was raising her himself was sometimes hard even for him to believe. But the fact that he'd also burdened himself with a twenty-five-thousand-dollar loan from his father to pay Tiffany Bates to carry Tanni to term would surely sound crazy to a practical, mature woman like Kitt. It would sound crazy until she met Tanni, that is.

"Here's an idea," Kitt said as she ran a finger over the five o'clock shadow on his jaw. "Why don't we all meet for the Fourth of July festivities on the Mall next week? I have to coordinate the Rally for Common Decency at one o'clock, but then I can arrange to be free later that evening. You and your friends could meet me somewhere, and we could have a picnic, watch the fireworks together."

Mark seized upon the low-key way to get Tanni

and Kitt together. Tanni and Carly would love it. The Mall, the fireworks, a picnic. It would be a fun way to get them all acquainted. And he could tell Kitt the whole story later, in private. He bent his head and kissed her hotly. ''Perfect,'' he said when he had thoroughly completed the job.

''My idea?'' Kitt said, pleasantly out of breath.

''No. The kiss.'' And he bent his head, found her mouth and demonstrated perfection again.

CHAPTER ELEVEN

REVEREND DALE WAS BEING excruciatingly long-winded.

Kitt tried to focus on his words, but the plain truth was she needed time to dash home before the rally to change clothes and pick up the apple pie she had slaved over last night. She often suffered the reverend's sermons for the sake of the benefits the First Baptist Church offered—the music, the fellowship, the teaching.

Today Kitt was particularly anxious to be gone.

Kitt had no illusions that making the dessert was anything but an irrational attempt to impress these special friends of Mark's, whoever they were. Weaseling out of the effectiveness assessment meeting after the rally this afternoon was one thing, but baking a pie? No doubt about it, this relationship had her by the nose.

She fidgeted on the hard pew. *Put a cork in it, Reverend Dale.* Her eyes wandered from the pulpit and caught the glance of the bouncy young woman from the young-adult Sunday-school class, Carly—

somebody. She was sitting across the aisle with her little niece, Tanni, the same little girl Kitt met a few Sundays ago on her way to teach songs to the first-graders. Kitt grinned at Tanni, and the child's face widened in a precious smile, then she waved at Kitt with one tiny finger. What a little doll.

Kitt had noticed the child standing way down a long hall that led to nothing but storage. The poor little thing had just stood there, looking forlorn. Lost, Kitt had thought. She'd approached the little girl cautiously, not wanting to frighten her, and asked, "What are you looking for, honey?"

"The baffroom." The child's eyes darted about wildly and the little chin quivered, tears held bravely in check. When she looked up at Kitt again, her face brightened. "Hey! You're the lady who teaches singing!"

"Yes, I am, and the bathroom's this way." Kitt held out her hand and the little girl took it.

The child immediately relaxed and admitted, "I got lost."

"Well, this is a very big church," Kitt said. "Where's your mommy?"

"I don't have a mommy," the little girl replied. Kitt felt a pang of something like pity, something like guilt.

"Oh. I see. Then, where's your daddy?"

"He's at home working on his capooter. But my aunt Carly's here—in a big class."

"Oh. And, are you in Sunday school, too?"

"Yeah. I'm in Miss Jody's class."

"What's your name?"

"Tanni."

"Well, Tanni, here's the bathroom. Can you manage okay?"

"Aunt Carly always helps me fix my panty hose and wash my hands." Kitt suppressed a smile at the word *panty hose* for the little white tights. *Precious.* "Well, why don't I help you?" she said, and followed the child inside.

While Tanni was in the stall, Kitt wondered why Jody had sent a four-year-old to the bathroom alone in such a big church building. Maybe she didn't have enough help in that classroom. Maybe Kitt should volunteer. No. She couldn't spend so much time with the four-year-olds. Never the four-year-olds. Any age but that.

Then the little girl came out and Kitt turned on the water for her, helped her to dispense the soap and work up a lather. As the child massaged her hands with the warm soapy water, she looked up into Kitt's eyes with her huge brown ones and said, "I wish I had a mommy."

There was such heartfelt feeling on the little face that Kitt was unsure how to respond. For one moment there was only the sound of the water gurgling down the drain, then Kitt managed to say, "What happened to your mommy, honey?"

"Daddy said she was too young to take care of me. So she gave me all to Daddy."

"I see." Kitt bit her lip, feeling a sudden, and painful, empathy for the young woman who was not here to wash her own child's hands. "Well, if she was just too young, then it's not really your mommy's fault she's not with you, is it?"

The little girl shrugged, stuck her hands under the water, turned them side to side carefully. "My aunt Carly always makes me say a little prayer for my mommy, right after we pray for Grandma and Grandpa."

"Yes." Kitt closed her eyes. Had someone taught her own child to include Kitt in his prayers? "That's the best thing you can do." And Kitt suddenly found herself choking back tears.

She turned abruptly and jerked out some paper towels from the wall dispenser. "After all, your mommy did the best she could." When she'd regained her composure, she squatted in front of the little girl and started drying the tiny hands. "So, you just keep on praying for her, okay?"

The child brushed her palms together. "Okey-dokey," she said matter-of-factly.

"Now let's get you back to Miss Jody." Kitt took

the little hand again. It was warm and damp now, and Tanni gave her a happy squeeze.

And Kitt couldn't help herself. She had to wonder if her own child's hand would feel anything like this.

After that incident, Kitt had done some discreet checking and found out that Carly and Tanni were newcomers who came to church alone.

So, Kitt, Paige and Lauren made a concerted effort to reach out to Carly and Tanni at fellowship time. In an area of constant demographic flux, Kitt considered it a calling to extend such friendliness. But even more than that, there was something about Tanni that attracted her, that had touched her heart. And, she had to admit it, something that haunted her.

While teaching songs to the four-year-olds this morning—she'd been forced to fill in for another teacher—Kitt found that once again she couldn't take her eyes off Tanni. And not just because she was a beautiful child—there was the other thing.

Had life gone differently, had Kitt made better choices, her own child, about Tanni's age, would be with her now. But there were twelve other four-year-olds in Tanni's class who could also remind Kitt of her lost child. Why was she so attracted to this one?

She thought again of the story Tanni's aunt, Carly, had shared with Lauren about how the little girl's father was raising Tanni by himself, with his family's help.

From across the aisle, Kitt caught Tanni's eye again and winked at the child, remembering how Tanni had tugged on Carly's sleeve one Sunday when Carly and Kitt stood visiting.

"Come *on*, Carly," the child pleaded. "We still have to find Daddy's *tie*. It's Father's Day."

"You wouldn't know where I could buy a tie on a Sunday morning?" Carly had asked Kitt. "Tanni always buys her daddy ties for special occasions, but I've been so busy getting us settled that we haven't had time to go get one for Father's Day yet, and today's the day!"

Kitt had given Carly directions to Pentagon City Mall.

Kitt's thoughts turned to meeting up with Mark later today. They were getting closer with each passing day. At least she hadn't gone to bed with him yet—and wouldn't, she reminded herself. He was leaving Washington soon. But they'd come so dangerously close. The utter sensuality of their relationship, she knew, was weakening her resolve. Maybe it would be a good thing to have other people with them this evening.

Only last night they'd rented a paddleboat on the Tidal Basin, wedged a small picnic basket on the seat between them and slowly paddled past the Jefferson Memorial as the sun sank over the hills of Arlington.

When they stopped to let their legs rest she'd opened the basket and offered him a ham sandwich.

He'd watched her steadily while he ate, and then, with that same sincerity and directness that always took her breath away, he'd said, "You look so beautiful in this light."

She'd been gazing toward the Washington Monument and the Capitol dome, both glowing amber in the distance. She turned her head, and saw him regarding her with a smile of pure adoration.

He'd laid the remainder of the sandwich in the basket, then reached over and fanned her hair out into the golden light, openly admiring it. She smiled, feeling self-conscious and uninhibited all at once. Lifting one of her hands, he kissed it, then covered it with both of his own. "What would you say, Kitt Stevens," he said, letting his gaze travel over her face, "if I told you that I love you?"

Kitt's heart lifted in her chest, felt as if it were bursting. "I guess," she answered when she finally could breathe, "I'd say that I love you, too."

They'd crashed into each other's arms then, almost capsizing the flatbottomed boat as they kissed in a fierce seal of freshly admitted love.

It had all happened so fast.

She had lost control, answering his force with her own, with her mouth seeking. He groaned in response to the small cry she made in the back of her throat as his tongue probed deeper. She brought one thigh up beside his hip, pressed herself into him. She wanted to feel him, needed to. He clasped her leg and pressed it higher on his hip.

"I do love you," she whispered as he grazed his mouth lightly over hers.

"I love you, too," he murmured against her lips, "and I want to know everything about you, everything that goes on in your head. Everything. I want to… Let me make love to you. Tonight."

His hands were warm, gentle yet demanding. And they showed her, more than his words, how badly he wanted to know her. When he brought his mouth down on her tender, swollen lips again, the sensation rocked her and made her want to cry out "Yes!"

But instead of letting her body say yes, she broke the kiss and gasped for air, for strength, to do what she felt compelled to do.

He mistook her move as offering him greater access and planted firm, hot kisses down her exposed throat.

Just as his lips touched the hollow at the base of her neck, she managed to say in a strained, gulping voice, "Mark, listen. I can't."

His head came up. He studied her face. She squeezed her eyes shut and felt tears threaten.

He released her then, not abruptly, but gently, slowly, reluctantly. She opened her eyes and looked at his, flushed with passion, but also thoroughly confused.

"Why not?" he'd said quietly as he brushed her tears away with one finger. And then he gently pulled her back to his chest, and stroked her hair, and hugged her tightly. "Okay," he said in a lighter tone. "I'll admit this boat's a bit cramped."

But Kitt didn't even smile at his little joke. "I can't," she repeated. She shook her head, swiped at her eyes. "*We* can't."

The bewilderment in his face gave way to a deeply troubled frown. She turned away from the sight of it.

"Why not?" He waited a minute, and when there was no answer, he said, "Kitt, did someone—" he seemed to be choosing his words carefully "—hurt you?" He curled a gentle finger under her chin.

"No. I mean, yes, sort of." She hung her head, rubbed her tears away with her palms. She wanted so badly to be honest with him. "But that's all in the past. What you need to understand is that I have no intention of getting sexually involved before marriage, and I have very good reasons for feeling that way."

"I see," he said quietly. "That's okay."

"It is? I mean, you understand?" She really couldn't believe he did. Most men these days didn't.

"Of course." He smiled kindly. "You have to do what's right for *you*."

He had dropped the subject, but he'd seemed uneasy. As if he sensed a complicated undercurrent. He had hugged her, had said all the right soothing things, but she could tell, by his subdued mood, by the set of his shoulders, that he knew there was more to this than she was willing to share.

And she could tell that he was genuinely confused. Not only by her tears and by her refusal to consummate a passion that was so clearly right for both of them, but by underlying troubles that he could not grasp.

Why had she not simply told Mark the whole truth, right then and there? The truth about Danny and the aftermath that had made her swear—*swear*—never again. Then she worried, would she *ever* be ready to talk about that? Or was she already putting distance between herself and Mark, sabotaging this relationship as she had every other one since Danny?

And now, she feared, the line of sexual inevitability had been breached. And even though she knew she wasn't about to cross it, she also knew she wasn't ready to reveal the complex reasons, the hurts, that held her back. If she could stall, she reasoned with herself, everything would work out. Mark was leaving Washington in three weeks. After that, time would be on her side. He would return to Oklahoma to finish his degree and she would continue with her career and her crusade. They could get to know each

other from a safe distance. There would be a time
for everything if this relationship was meant to be.
Time for her to figure out a way to tell him her story.
Once she found a way to tell him, she felt certain he
would understand. *Then* they would find their way to
true intimacy. He was the kind of man who would
understand.

She felt suddenly hopeful. Nothing was going to
mess up this relationship. She wouldn't allow it.

She hadn't realized how tense these thoughts were
making her until her enormous sigh brought a judg-
mental look from an older woman sitting next to her
in the pew.

She tried to show renewed interest in the reverend's words, reminding herself that today was far
from that horrible day four years ago. Today she was
fine. Today she would meet Mark's friends. Share
apple pie and fireworks. Today she would have fun.

Reverend Dale was winding it up in the rounded
tones of an old-time preacher. "Awll of us, parents
or not, must make an effort to attend the Rally for
Common Decency on the Ellipse at one o'clock too-
day and join ow-er brothers and sisters from around
the country in demonstrating ow-er support for a
cleaner, safer culture for ow-er children."

Later, Kitt watched Paige and Lauren work the
crowd during coffee and doughnuts in the fellowship
center. Ignoring the juice in their disposable cups,

they shook hands with young and old, picking up last-minute recruits for the rally. "Two buses will leave the parking lot at noon," she heard Lauren explain repeatedly. "Be there or be square," Paige would add.

Out of the corner of her eye, Kitt spotted Carly, visiting with a group of young women.

She crossed the room, signaling Carly aside. "Are you coming to the rally?"

"I'll be there," Carly assured her, "no matter what my thick-headed big brother says."

"Oh? And what does your brother say?"

"He doesn't want me to go. He says it's not safe for Tanni to be at some radical political rally—"

"Radical?" Kitt didn't appreciate this brother's labels. The people who supported the cause of responsible media came from all walks of life. "Trying to protect this country's children is *not* radical—"

Just then Tanni skipped over. "Hurry *up,* Aunt Carly." The child yanked on Carly's skirt. "We have to get the picnic ready for the *fireworks* at the Mall!"

"All right, honey, as soon as I'm finished talking to Kitt." Carly turned her attention back to Kitt. "I suspect what he's really worried about is me and Tanni getting in his way while he's working. He's a reporter—covering the rally for his precious *Dallas Morning News.*"

"Really?" was all Kitt could say, because something horribly unsettling was chewing at the edges of her mind.

She looked down at Tanni, who stood waiting beside Carly, sporting an impatient pout while she picked at a tiny hangnail. With fresh eyes, Kitt noted again the child's dark, dark hair, lying in a certain familiar pattern. The perfect little nose with its faint sprinkle of freckles. The full mouth.

But Kitt pushed the idea away, wouldn't even allow herself to question Carly. Mark would have told her if he had a daughter, for heaven's sake. He was the most honest man she had ever met. And thousands, she told herself, *thousands* of people would be on the Mall for the Fourth of July festivities tonight. It was all a huge coincidence. It could not be anything else. It simply could not be.

CHAPTER TWELVE

IT WAS HOT. It was noisy. It was dumb.

But Mark tried to remain professional. To remain objective and impartial and accurate. But these people were so damn irritating.

Take the tennis balls. Police barricades had been erected in anticipation of the crowd, which was considerable, keeping them at an ineffective distance from the White House. But the main body of protesters had come prepared for this tactic. They'd brought fluorescent-colored tennis balls, ink-markered with potent messages. They lobbed the balls past the barricades and over the chain-link fence beyond in a periodic rain of lime green, neon yellow and hot orange. It was a media moment for sure. A great visual stunt for the cameras. Smart. No doubt a Kitt trick.

Kitt had done a heck of a job stirring these people up, that's for sure. Joan of Arc against the evil media beast.

He smiled, remembering the surge of love and pride he felt as he watched her perform before the massive crowd, a diverse mixture of parents, educators, pediatricians, psychologists, social workers, concerned churchgoers, along with a large contingent of teenage activists who'd been bussed in from schools affected by recent violence. Gun control activists had shown up as well, which had in turn drawn the "right to bear arms" crowd onto the opposite corner. A smattering of videogamers were there with signs, protecting their "right to excitement." And on the periphery, a collection of outcasts Mark couldn't identify. All assembled with banners and signs on the Ellipse, ready to march on the White House…or against each other.

"Ms. Stevens!" He'd signaled from the back tier of the press bleachers. When he got her attention, he'd briefly enjoyed her shocked look of recognition—his reward for not telling her he'd be covering *her* rally. "Now that you've focused so much media attention on your cause, Ms. Stevens, what are your plans after this rally?" The double meaning of his question was entirely intentional. Her plans after the rally included *him,* of course.

She stared at him and her face shot red, became mottled in fact, but her voice was steady as it echoed out over the sound system. "We intend to continue to take this issue directly to the American public," she said without once faltering. "And keep it there. This rally is only the beginning of what we hope will be a cultural reversal. We will use whatever means necessary to restore decency and common sense to our media. For example, we'll boycott sponsors of violent, lewd programming. We will not give up this fight for the protection of our children's hearts and minds!''

The crowd roared at that and the cameras rolled obligingly. His love and pride quadrupled later, when he saw her mingling with the protesters as they lined up to march. People responded to her leadership, huddled around her, hung on her every word. She really knew how to do her job.

And so did he. Ever picky about facts, and wanting to get the messages on the tennis balls verbatim, Mark pushed through the crowd, determined to retrieve one for himself.

He made it past the barricades along with a few energetic teenagers, and right up to the chain-link fence. No hope of grabbing one of the incoming missiles: too high, too fast. He had succeeded in talking one of the security guards into handing him a ball through the fence just as the other guards, apparently fed up with the crowd's little game, started pitching the balls back over. The crowd instantly returned fire, hurling the tennis balls like a shower of live grenades, chanting louder and louder: Clean up our culture! Clean up our culture!

And Mark got his tennis ball all right—smack in

the back of the head. He didn't even have the consolation of grabbing it to see what it said.

"Ouch!" he yelled as he rubbed his skull and retreated with some of the others who'd been hit.

He continued to massage the sore spot as the screaming crowd surged around him. Things had suddenly turned agitated, ugly. Thank God Tanni and Carly were nowhere near this mess. Now he only had to worry about Kitt.

Then he spotted her, weaving around people, forging her way forward, right into the heart of the fray. "Kitt!" he yelled as he shoved his way toward her. She turned, searching the faces in the crowd. He reached her side before she saw him. "Don't go up there!" he shouted, and grabbed her arm, spinning her around. She had a bullhorn clasped in one hand. "The guards and the crowd are losing control."

She stared at him, then down at the hand squeezing her arm. "What are *you* doing here?"

He released his grip. "My job," he said simply. "I'm sorry I didn't tell you I was covering this—"

"Why didn't you?" She seemed angry.

"I don't know. Maybe I thought you'd avoid me or something. It seems like, when it comes to this stuff—" he flung his arm out and it bumped a yelling bystander "—like you see me as the enemy...or something."

"I do not!"

Having to keep their voices raised to be heard above the crowd made it feel as if their argument was escalating faster than it should have.

"Look. I'm just doing my job." He tried to sound calm.

"Well this is *my* job." Her gaze shifted wildly to the side, where protesters were breaking ranks at the curb and running across the grass. "I have to get these people calmed down before somebody gets hurt!"

"Let the police do that!" Two teenage boys to his left were screaming so loudly that Mark could hardly hear himself above their hoarse voices. "Would you shut the hell up!" Mark turned on them. When he turned back toward her, Kitt was gone. She had melted into the crowd. "Damn!" he yelled, and rubbed the back of his still-smarting head.

Kitt battled the jostling bodies around her, intent on reaching a rise in front of the chain-link fence. She prayed the crowd would recognize her and calm down as she pleaded for order. But suddenly she lost all interest in crowd control as she caught sight of something that sickened her. Carly, running down the street, against the crowd, with Tanni riding her hip, tripped and stumbled forward. While Kitt watched in horror, Carly took a nosedive to the pavement and landed on top of Tanni.

Kitt didn't know how she reached them so fast,

but Carly hadn't even made it to her feet before Kitt got to their side. A couple of graying ladies in tennis shoes were bent forward, helping them stand up. Tanni was crying hard and a large purple egg was already forming right in the middle of her forehead.

"Are you okay?" Kitt shouted above the noise.

"I am, but Tanni's hurt." Carly's face, beet-red from the heat, was stricken with worry. Kitt glanced down. Both of Carly's knees were badly scraped.

"Let me see, sweetie." Kitt stooped to examine the crying child's forehead. "We need to get this looked at," she said decisively. "I'll carry Tanni." Kitt picked the child up, adjusted her on her hip. "You're going to be all right, sweetie," she said, patting her. "Can you keep up?" she asked Carly.

Carly nodded and they took off. "Where are we going?" she said.

"George Washington University Hospital. About six blocks that way."

Kitt hoisted the bullhorn and ordered the crowd out of the way, then she broke into a trot as she cut across the grassy Ellipse toward Pennsylvania Avenue. She figured she couldn't get the attention of the policemen in front of the White House. They were too busy with crowd control. She kept an anxious eye out for a taxi but because of the rally, the traffic was dense beyond belief.

What a mess, Kitt thought as she continued to run

the endless blocks in the punishing heat. The protesters becoming disorderly. Tanni getting hurt. Mark
showing up.

Mark.

The pieces were falling into place faster than a row
of tumbling dominoes. If this was true—she hugged
Tanni tighter to her side—*if* this was his child, their
situation was too ironic to contemplate. Mark had a
child exactly the age of hers. Why hadn't he told her?
She hadn't confronted him a moment ago, not here,
not now, because she hoped it wasn't true.

Tanni, who had quieted the minute Kitt picked her
up, felt like a humid little lump against Kitt's shoulder. A surge of concern washed through Kitt. Was
the little girl so subdued because something was ter-
ribly wrong? A concussion? The traffic gridlock
never did clear up, and Kitt, with pounding heart and
burning lungs, ended up carrying the child all the
way to the emergency room door.

KITT HAD NEVER had the pleasure of waiting anxiously in a major metropolitan emergency room. And
this one was jammed with casualties from the rally.
The thing that struck her as almost hysterical was a
sign, posted above the nurses' station window,
broadcasting in foot-high red letters: QUIET. With
sirens wailing, kids crying and staff shouting, this
place was anything but.

The lights were too bright, bearing down like miniature suns. The hospital smells...antiseptics, linen,
paper scrubs, mixed with the stench of fear and
sweat.

The only other time she'd been in a hospital, her
maternity room had seemed deathly quiet, filled with
the hushed sound of finality, the misplaced timbre of
sorrow, in an otherwise happy ward. To keep herself
from thinking about her past, which seemed freshly
painful now, she refocused on Tanni and Carly. It
was a good thing she'd been nearby when Carly fell.
She felt responsible for all of this!

Carly was standing over Tanni's gurney now, anxiously studying the tiny face. Kitt went to the other
side of the gurney, hoping to persuade Carly to sit
for a spell. From the looks of the chaos in this E.R.,
they were in for a long wait.

Without looking up, Carly raised a finger to her
lips. Tanni's eyes had drifted closed.

"Why don't you sit down?" Kitt whispered.

Tanni's eyes popped open. "Would you sing me
a song, Miss Kitt? Please?" she implored.

"Sure, honey," Kitt murmured. Carly nodded and
went to the chair and Kitt carefully smoothed Tanni's
hair away from her injured forehead with two light
fingers while she sang a little preschool song to her.

At first Kitt was relieved to see how her humming
soothed Tanni, but a new worry occurred to her as

she watched Tanni's eyelids drift closed and the small chest rise and fall with ever-deepening respirations. Was it okay for her to go to sleep? And was the giant purple bump on her head getting bigger?

Kitt dived around the green curtain that housed them in their cubicle, looking wildly for a nurse. She grabbed a yellow paper sleeve as it flew by. "Nurse! She keeps going to sleep! Is that okay? Is that normal?"

The nurse stopped. In one hand she clutched a rolling IV pole, in the other some sort of sterilely wrapped tray, a plastic bag of blood balanced on top of that. "Who, hon?" she said with undisguised impatience.

"Tanni. The little girl…in here." Kitt jerked at the paper gown, ripping the shoulder. "Sorry. The one who hit her head on the pavement. She keeps going to sleep. Please. You have to check her."

The nurse gave her sleeve a disdainful glance, then peered past the curtain at the tiny body on the gurney. "Has she been seen by a doctor?"

"No! No one's seen her but the triage nurse, and we've been here for forty minutes already, and I think that bump's getting bigger!"

The nurse grimaced. "Okay. Let me check her pupils." She parked the IV pole, tossed the tray and the bag at the foot of Tanni's gurney and whipped out a penlight while Kitt murmured a thank-you.

The nurse leaned over Tanni and said, "Tanni? We've got to check your eyes, okay?" She pried Tanni's eye open, shining the light in. Tanni fought the intrusion, but the nurse pressed her weight across the child and mumbled, "I know, baby, almost done," as she repeated the procedure on the other eye. Then she walked to the foot of the stretcher, snapped up the chart and wrote.

Kitt peered over the nurse's shoulder. "P.E.R.L." the nurse wrote next to the time, then initialed the entry.

"P.E.R.L.? Is she okay?" Kitt whispered. Across the cubicle, Carly remained pale and silent, as she had been since they'd arrived.

"She's fine," the nurse said as she gathered her supplies. "Pupils are reactive, equal. That bump's all on the outside. Better put that ice back on it, though." She nodded toward a blue cold pack that Tanni had pushed away. "Let her sleep. We're filled to the max because of that crowd at the Ellipse, but we'll check her again in fifteen minutes." The curtain flapped and the nurse was gone.

Kitt let out a whoosh of air, then picked up the cold pack. "Tanni, honey, you need this to make your head better." She clumsily wrapped the pack in a washcloth, then gently laid it over the injured area.

Tanni's face puckered in a pout and she skewered

Kitt with irate little eyes. "I want my daddy," she insisted.

Kitt looked to Carly for support and, at last, Carly broke her frightened silence. "I know you do, honey." She stood and reached over to pat Tanni's hand. "Daddy will be here soon."

After she bent and kissed Tanni's cheek, she raised her eyes to Kitt. "I've paged Mark twice, he should be calling here soon."

Mark.

As soon as Carly said it, the name fell through Kitt's mind like a stone, landing in her deepest well of fear. Somehow she managed to say, "That's her daddy's name? Mark?" in a normal voice.

Kitt had carried Tanni around into the cubicle, had stayed with her while Carly hurried to fill out paperwork and provide vital information. Information like that all-important name. Mark.

Carly nodded, put a finger to her lips again, signaling that Tanni was drifting off. Kitt was relieved to be silenced because she was afraid of what she might say...or what she might be told.

She had plenty of time to think about the implications while they waited for Mark. She timed the agony by Tanni's pupil checks. As the nurse promised, someone came to do a check every fifteen minutes. Every time they woke Tanni she requested another song, then drifted to sleep halfway through it. Just after a young male nurse completed the second check, when Kitt had started singing "My Favorite Things," Mark appeared at the gap in the curtains.

"Daddy!" Tanni's voice chirped. "You found me!"

Mark darted to Tanni, and Kitt could see only her little feet sticking up under the sheet as he enveloped his child in a shielding hug. She stared at that massive back as it strained the fabric of his sweat-soaked chambray shirt. That was the back she had come to love so much, along with everything else about him.

"Daddy, we been having a 'venture!" Tanni's voice piped from beneath him.

He mumbled something so softly that Kitt could not make it out, then looked over his shoulder. "Kitt?" he said quietly. "What are you doing here?"

"That's Miss Kitt, my Sunday-school music teacher!" Tanni informed him, getting more alert and excited by the minute.

"Oh, is she?" Mark's voice remained as soothing as balm.

"Yes! And she was there when I bonked my head!" Tanni popped the side of her forehead to demonstrate, and Mark gently took her little hand down. "And then she runned with me—a long ways—and it was so *hot,* Daddy!"

"It was faster than taking a cab, with all the congestion from the rally..." Kitt's voice faltered when Mark turned to look at her. Dear God. Mark is Tanni's father. Mark has a *child*. Why hadn't he told her?

"I can't thank you enough for taking care of my baby." Mark turned back to Tanni. "Well, that sounds *bad*, princess—" Mark smoothed back her hair "—but you're okay now. And guess what? Daddy got bonked by a tennis ball! But his old head is too hard to get hurt."

Tanni giggled.

"Now, the nurse said you should rest, so just close those little eyes." He frowned at the bruise on her forehead as he continued his gentle petting.

When he had soothed Tanni back to sleep, Mark straightened and his gaze zeroed in on the sign propped in the corner, the one that Carly had distractedly carried with her all the way from the rally. It read: A Mind Is a Terrible Thing To Trash. The bullhorn was propped next to it.

Kitt saw a muscle work in his jaw before he whispered to Carly, "Could I speak to you a moment—in private?"

There was nothing private about it. They went around the curtain and Kitt could hear their voices clearly. Mark's angry one was first.

"An adventure, huh? What in the hell were you

doing at that ridiculous rally? I thought I told you to stay home!''

''Don't you talk to me like that!'' Kitt heard Carly respond. ''I was there because I *care* what happens to kids. Besides, this is a free country!'' Her voice carried above the emergency room racket. ''You make a pretty mean freedom-of-speech speech, Mark Masters, until somebody disagrees with you. You're starting to sound just like Dad!''

''I don't sound anything like Dad!'' He lowered his voice. ''And that rally had nothing to do with freedom of speech—''

''Well, step on my face and feed me a bug,'' Carly interrupted sarcastically, ''but that's exactly what it was about! Decent people have the right to express their opinions, too, you know!''

Mark's voice rose again, and Kitt could hear the barely controlled anger in it. ''Car-lee, why do you always talk in stupid platitudes? What this is about is, Tanni might have a concussion because you dragged her to a confrontational, potentially danger-ous demonstration against my wishes!''

''Daddy! Don't yell!'' a sleepy little voice admon-ished from the gurney. Kitt winced.

Mark's contrite face appeared around the curtain. ''I'm sorry, sweetheart.'' He blew her a kiss.

Kitt patted Tanni's hand and adjusted the ice pack, then gave Mark a chastising look. Oh, would she like to give him a piece of her mind when Carly was through with him.

Mark closed the curtain and Kitt heard him say, albeit more quietly, "You're lucky all I'm doing is yelling at you, Carly. How dare you drag Tanni to that spectacle and get her injured. The plain fact is, Tanni got hurt because you didn't listen to me. The doctor said they were holding her for observation, that it was probably nothing to worry about, but it could have been." There was a meaningful pause. "It could have been."

"I know." Kitt thought she heard the beginnings of tears in Carly's voice.

"Come here," Mark said gently. "Hey, don't cry," he said. "It's okay. Tanni's okay."

After a minute, Carly's muffled voice asked, "You know Kitt?"

"Well, yeah. But I had no idea you did. Here."

Kitt heard Carly blowing her nose, then, "It was a good thing she was nearby when Tanni got hit. She was great. She goes to my church, you know."

"Really?" Mark's voice now had the sound of one absorbing a delightful surprise.

"Yeah, she teaches music at Sunday school," Carly elaborated. "How do you know her?"

"Well, you're not going to believe this, little sister, but Kitt's the woman I've been dating."

There was a silence that seemed interminable to

Kitt, then, "Well, alleluia. For once you are dating a respectable woman." And, for reasons known only to Kitt, Carly's innocent joke made Kitt's face flame red and her heart contract with fear. *A respectable woman?* Would Carly really think so if she knew about Kitt's past?

When Mark came back around the curtain, he crossed the cubicle and hugged Kitt's shoulders tenderly. "Kitt?" he said. "Thank you for helping my girls."

"Your girls," Kitt echoed flatly. "Carly is your sister...and Tanni is your daughter?"

Feeling her body stiffen, Mark released her. "Yes. And it looks like you already know them from your church," he said. "What a crazy coincidence, huh? But still, it's really, really neat." And he meant it. He had warmed to the idea, already thinking that fate had ordained this. "Isn't it a small world?" he added.

"Mark, I—"

"So, you've been dating Mark!" Carly interrupted, looking as pleased by this coincidence as her brother. She placed a confidential touch on Kitt's arm. "I never dreamed you two were dating."

"Isn't it a small world?" Mark repeated.

Tanni peeked at Kitt; she hadn't been sleeping after all. "Miss Kitt," she said. "Are you going on the picnic with me and Aunt Carly and my daddy?"

Kitt had to struggle to speak. Underneath her shock and fear, she felt a very real anger. What was Mark planning to do at the picnic? Pass her off to his family as a casual friend, as he had them to her? But what could she do now with that innocent pair of brown eyes pleading with her? "Yes. I am." She smiled at Tanni, too brightly, she knew.

Tanni smiled back and clapped her hands.

Mark beamed at both of them, but when he caught Kitt's glance, he reverted to caution. "I don't know about any picnic. First, we have to see what the doctor says."

Selfishly, Kitt hoped the doctor said no. Because all she could think at that moment was: How can I pretend to enjoy a picnic when I feel as if I've just been run over by a truck?

"But Daddy—" Before Tanni could argue, a sudden commotion outside the cubicle curtain distracted them. A nurse was explaining in high tones how busy the staff was.

"I understand," a deep voice boomed. "Now, if you'll just get that doctor." Suddenly the curtain was thrust aside. There stood an older silver-haired version of Mark. Tall, broad-shouldered, wearing a finely tailored double-breasted suit.

"Granddad!" Tanni shrieked and tossed away the ice pack as she knelt up on the gurney and stretched forth her arms.

The tall man's face spread into a smile as he stepped into the cubicle and lifted Tanni, squeezing her to his chest. His expensive aftershave pervaded the small space. "How's my punkin?" he said as he telegraphed Mark a worried look over the child's head.

"It's just a bump, Dad," Mark said evenly, "but I think she should lie down until the doctor says otherwise." As he pried Tanni's skinny arms from around the tall man's neck, the little girl cried, "No! I want Granddad to hold me!"

"Then you have to be still," the child's grandfather warned, and propped one hip on the gurney while he settled Tanni onto his lap.

Mark backed up a step and folded his arms across his chest. His mouth smiled at Tanni, but his eyes didn't look happy.

"She needs this, Dad." Carly stepped forward with the ice pack.

"Hello, sweetheart, give Daddy a kiss." He took the ice pack and put a clean-shaved cheek forward for Carly.

Carly obliged. She kept a hand on his shoulder as she turned toward Kitt and said, "Dad, this is Kitt—"

"I know who Ms. Stevens is. But I can't quite figure out what she's doing here."

"I was at the rally."

"She's my friend."

"Kitt and Mark are dating."

All had spoken at once.

"I was just about to ask you what *you* are doing here," Mark said.

But the old man ignored the question and looked Kitt up and down. *"Dating?"*

Kitt sensed so many unspoken messages zinging around the tiny space that she could hardly process them all. Mark and his father competing over Tanni. Carly trying to be a peacemaker. Mark not wanting his father here. Marcus Masters not approving of Kitt.

"Dad—" Mark started.

"It's a pleasure to meet you at last, Mr. Masters." Kitt stepped forward. "I've heard so many things about you while I've worked on this legislation." *Wasn't life just strange as hell?* a rebellious little part of her mind mused. This was certainly not the way she would have ever imagined her first meeting with her most virulent enemy. And this was most certainly not the way she would have imagined meeting the family of the love of her life. She extended her hand.

Masters took it, and his grip was very much like Mark's: strong, warm, confident. "Likewise, Ms. Stevens. That was your little rally out there, wasn't it? Your brainstorm?"

"Well, I organized it. But the people who cared enough to show up made it happen."

"Miss Stevens, in my experience, the people don't know what they want until somebody tells them. But from what I saw on TV in the limo, your little upstart organization will get ample press out of this nonsense."

Mark had retreated to the edge of the cubicle and was pinching the bridge of his nose as if he had a killer headache. Carly sat in the lone chair, her shoulders slumped. Everybody but Tanni, who was dozing, seemed tense as a guy wire.

"Dad," Mark said without looking up, "how did you ever find us?"

Carly and her father exchanged a guilty look.

"Phil informed me."

"Phil?" Mark frowned. "Who's Phil?"

Marcus cleared his throat. "I've hired a...an attendant for Carly and Tanni while they are living in D.C."

"An attendant? You mean a bodyguard?"

"Surely you don't think I'd let them run around urban D.C. without protection," Marcus glanced at Tanni's sleeping face and kept his voice low.

Mark shot Carly a questioning look.

"He's nice enough." Carly shrugged. "And he keeps his distance."

Suddenly Kitt remembered a tall, balding man

with a trim mustache whom she'd seen in the background, once at church and again at the rally…watching Carly and Tanni. If so much hadn't happened at once, she would have asked Carly about him, possibly even reported him.

"Yes," Marcus growled. "And we'll be addressing that. Apparently he was too far away to be of any use when Tanni got injured."

"It's not his fault." Carly explained. "I panicked and forgot all about him."

"Actually, it was my fault." Kitt stepped up. "I scooped Tanni up and ran with her when I saw how fast that bump was forming."

"Kitt took good care of us, Dad," Carly defended.

Mark's jaw had tightened and now he turned on his father. "You never give up, do you? I tell you I'm going to live my life my way, and you just keep sending your goons to spy."

"Mark!" Carly snapped. "Phil is nice. He's a retired Texas Ranger—"

"Spy?" Marcus hissed. "People with far fewer assets than I have, have had…incidents. You're forgetting about Robbie Werner's kidnapping."

Mark rolled his eyes and planted his hands at his belt, staring at the floor. "I can never reason with you," he muttered.

"D.C. is a very dangerous town. Just look at this."

Marcus frowned down at the bump on Tanni's forehead.

"How'd you get here so fast? Have you been hovering over National Airport in your Lear, waiting for an *incident* to happen?"

"Sarcastic as always. It just so happens I flew in from Philadelphia this morning for the purposes of observing this rally. The outcome of this thing had Wilkens mighty nervous. This kind of trumped-up grassroots thing could cost us a couple of key congressional votes." Marcus shot a look at Kitt as if this whole disaster were her fault.

Definitely not, she decided, the greatest way to get acquainted with your boyfriend's family.

The doctor swooped in and the cubicle seemed unbearably congested.

"Maybe I should go to the waiting room," Kitt offered, and slipped out.

No sooner had she seated herself in one of the hard plastic chairs than Carly appeared.

"Dad's a pain," she said as she settled herself into the chair beside Kitt. "But he means well. Ignore him. He thinks anybody who doesn't agree with him is either a Communist or somehow mentally impaired."

Kitt smiled. "What did the doctor say about Tanni?"

"I didn't stay long enough to hear. But I'm sure

Dad and Mark will find a way to argue about it, whatever he says. One will say black and one will say white, and off they'll go.''

"They're always like that?"

Carly nodded.

"And does your dad get under your skin, too?"

"Sometimes."

"Mark told me your mother is deceased. You must miss her."

Carly's expression became bittersweet. "I do. But I still love her and try to be like her. You know what I mean?"

Kitt patted Carly's hand. "I wish I did know. My mother died when I was only eight. I don't remember much about her, but now that I think about it, I do remember the love I felt for her, and I guess I always will."

"Oh, Kitt. I'm sorry. Your mom's dead, too? And eight is so young, not much older than Tanni. But at least you do remember what it felt like to love her. And it's remembering the love that counts, isn't it?"

Kitt studied the girl. "Carly, how'd you get to be so wise and mature at such a young age?"

Carly smiled. "You wouldn't have to ask if you'd ever met my mother."

"Mark said she was special."

Carly nodded, then stared off into space with the same lost look on her face that Mark had when he talked about his mother. As she studied the girl's profile, Kitt couldn't believe the resemblance, couldn't believe she hadn't seen it. But, of course, she hadn't been looking for something so wildly co-incidental.

"I can hardly believe you're Mark's sister and that—"

"That he has a little girl?" Carly guessed.

"Yeah." Kitt frowned. "I can't believe he didn't tell me about her."

"Don't be hurt, and don't be too hard on him. He's very protective of Tanni. It hasn't been easy on him, being a single parent."

"I can imagine," Kitt said. But that was the trouble. She couldn't imagine. Four years ago she hadn't even allowed herself to imagine it. Hadn't even tried.

"THIS IS *SO COO-UHL*," Carly had gushed later that afternoon as she pulled the picnic basket from the trunk of the Lexus.

There they were, all of them, pretending to be extremely pleased at this unexpected turn of events. All of them virtually overflowing with happiness about being together. All of them except Marcus Masters. And Kitt.

Exactly how she had made it through that endless evening, Kitt could never say. Choking down the picnic food while Mark and Marcus kept up their sub-

terranean struggle. Enduring Tanni's unbridled childish affection—she closed her eyes as she thought of
how Tanni had skipped up to hold her hand, making
a bridge between Kitt and Mark. Smiling on cue at
Carly's wry teenage wisecracks and upbeat attitude,
and, worst of all, witnessing Mark's painful conflict.
She could practically read his thoughts: *Great! My
sister and my daughter clearly like Kitt and, pre-
dictably, my old man clearly doesn't.*

Beneath his gentlemanly veneer, Marcus Masters
was treating Kitt like the harlot spy from the enemy
camp. The man even had the nerve to ask about
Trisha Pounds in front of Kitt.

"Never saw her again after the ice-cream social.
Never called her," Mark said, and took a big, defiant
bite of chicken.

But even worse than the older Masters's cool in-
civility were moments like the one when Tanni had
said, "Hey, Kitt, my daddy wore his good-luck tie
today." She pointed at the tie, which Mark had discarded on the blanket. Patterned with children's stick
figures, silly and inappropriate, like all the other ties
he wore. Kitt's heart had actually hurt, remembering
the day he'd flapped his tie at her when they first
met. *Tanni* was the "girl with impeccable taste" in
his life. *Tanni* was the innocent wedge that doomed
their relationship, much more so than some other

woman like Trisha Pounds could, more than any domineering, disapproving father could.

Because Kitt was convinced that Mark could never love her once he learned the truth about the decision she had made at almost the same time that he was struggling to raise his child on his own. No. Never. He would never understand.

The lively Sousa music, the happy families in Bermuda shorts, the taste of her own apple pie, all seemed to underscore for Kitt one deadening realization—Mark Masters, of all men, would never understand her decision to give away her own child.

And then, during the fireworks, Tanni had crawled from her father's lap onto Kitt's lap. And Kitt had sat there hugging the little body and smelling the sweet scent of a child's hair, and feeling the warmth of that child's father's palm through the back of her shirt...and wanting to die.

ALONE IN HER BED that night, Kitt let the tears come. This time she had begun to think it was really going to be okay. This time she had let herself fall in love with a man, thinking—foolishly—that her past was behind her...but this time...how could she ever be a mother to Tanni? She had not even been able to be a mother to her own child.

Early in the morning—before she could change her mind—she called Mark and told him that they couldn't see each other anymore. There was a pause and then in a sleepy voice, he asked her to "say that again." When she did—slowly, carefully so that there would be no mistaking her resolve—he hung up.

It seemed only seconds before she heard the roar of the Kawasaki out on the street in front of the town house. He pounded on her door until it sounded as if it might crack.

"Who on earth is banging on the door like that?" Lauren said as she sprinted from the kitchen toward the door. She shot Kitt an irritated look as she tightened the sash of her robe.

Kitt stopped Lauren before she opened the door. "It's Mark."

"Oh." Lauren was suddenly subdued.

Mark pummeled the door again, and Lauren retreated upstairs. As soon as Kitt opened the door, he started yelling at her through the face shield of the helmet, then grabbed the chinbar and gave it a vicious jerk up. "Kitt," he said. He was breathing hard, breathing fire, and his eyes were like angry blue lasers. "What the—" His voice cracked, and she had to turn away at the sight of the pain in his eyes. "What the *hell*—" His voice cracked again and he swallowed. "What the hell do you mean? Saying we can't see each other anymore?"

"We're not right for each other, Mark."

CHAPTER THIRTEEN

MARK DROPPED the helmet on bricks, and it bounced down the narrow steps. Without another word, he grabbed her by the shoulders and fastened his mouth onto hers, thrusting in his tongue, crushing her to his chest, all in one swift motion.

Kitt fought to keep her eyes open. She tried to focus on the tree outside the door, on the sunlight, on the sound of the morning birds. She resisted, with all her will, the pull of that kiss.

When the kiss was over, he wrapped his body around hers. Through her thin robe, she could feel his strength, his male need, plainly, as he used it without shame to speak directly to her, thigh to thigh, belly to belly, heart to heart. "Tell me what's not right about this," he whispered near her ear.

"We have other things to consider...other people."

"If you're talking about Tanni... I'm so sorry," he breathed against her hair as he bent over her. "I should have told you about Tanni. I should have..."

He should have told her about Tanni? My God, he

thinks I'm breaking it off because he's a single father! Kitt tried to free herself from his embrace. She had to make him see that this was simply not true, that the problem wasn't with Tanni, it was with Kitt. Tanni deserved a real mother, not some woman who was terrified of that role, who had turned away from her own chance at it. Feeling defeated, she laid her cheek against the warm folds of his T-shirt. "Tanni—"

"Kitt," he interrupted, "you don't have to say anything. I understand. I know you better than that. I know this isn't just because Tanni exists. If you *were* breaking up with me because I have a child, you wouldn't be the woman I fell in love with. I wouldn't want you."

She could only shake her head.

He tightened his arms. "I meant—" he stopped and drew a huge breath "—I wouldn't blame you for being upset with me because I didn't tell you about Tanni sooner. I was waiting to tell you because…I don't know. You've got to realize that this child of mine is all I had…until I met you."

"Don't say that." She didn't want him elevating her to the same category as his beloved child. Not now. Not when she couldn't even bring herself to tell him her terrible secret.

He squeezed her harder. "It's true. But I realize there's something—I *hope* there's something else—

and let's be honest, my dad would scare off any sane person.''

She shook her head against his shoulder again and tried to move back, to create a space between them.

He rushed on, his words firing out at hyper-speed. ''There is something else. I knew it when we were out on the Tidal Basin the other night. Whatever it is, whatever is wrong, *whatever* is holding you back, it isn't enough to give up on what we have.''

Kitt went limp. The truth of his words, his willingness to fight for their relationship, the sheer power and heat and urgency of his wonderful body—all of it was overwhelming.

He let out a rush of air, relaxed his grip, pressed his forehead to hers, started over. ''Kitt, listen, we're just getting started here, and whatever is wrong, we can work it out.'' He said this quietly, reasonably. ''I want you to be mine. And I want to be yours. I want us to be... *Us*—''

She could feel him looking down at her again. ''Listen to me. I have *never* loved a woman the way I love you—'' His voice broke on the last two words. He waited a moment, then he sounded strong, sure again. ''Look, I could tell it was a shock when you found out about Tanni, and I know my dad can be a real jerk, but...'' He gave her shoulders another little shake. ''Whatever is in our way—Tanni, or my father, or money, or politics—it doesn't matter. In the end this is about you and me. We can make it work.''

While he had been saying all these things, she had managed not to look into his face. But now that he was silent she raised her eyes and wished she hadn't. His mouth, pale and tight, was turned down at the corners as if he was sealing in more unspoken words, more unexpressed feelings. His eyes were closed and it looked as if he might be fighting back tears. The man she had thought so young looking when she had first seen him did not look young at all at this moment. He looked every inch a mature man—a man in pain, desperate. She swallowed hard and thought, *How can I do this to him?*

He opened his eyes—they were bloodshot from the strain of holding back tears—and looked into hers. "I'll tell you one thing. I promise *I* won't keep anything from you." He brought his mouth down on hers, whispered, "Ever," against her lips just before he kissed her with a kiss that conveyed all the meaning of everything that he had been saying, all that he was promising.

And the absolute rightness of his kiss made Kitt want to die. His taste, sweet and hot, blended with the bitter saltiness of her tears. He'd been so honest with her. But there was, she felt, no truth in herself to offer back.

She had given away her child. He still had his. He

had made one set of choices. She had made another. That was the truth. That was the difference between them. Not his father or money or politics. Even if she told him that truth, she was convinced that he'd be done with her anyway. So, she could either live a lie and keep her past secret or expose herself as something he would abhor, or worse, pity. Either way, she would lose him. Either way, Mark Masters would not love the real Kitt Stevens. She broke off the kiss, shook her head again violently, and pushed him away.

He dropped his arms and stood before her as if all life had suddenly drained from him. The pain and confusion in his face was so raw she wanted to turn her face, to run from it.

"No," she said more softly, more apologetically than before. "This relationship can't work, Mark." She swiped at her tears and looked down so she would not have to see the look in his eyes. "For reasons you can't understand."

But he forced her to look at him by bending his knees and positioning his face under hers. "Why do you keep saying that?" he said in a tone of complete desperation. "You're wrong! Not only can it work, it could be beautiful. Glorious! If I believe that, why can't you?"

She twisted her shoulders and ducked her head away from him. "Because you don't know what you're talking about. I have...complications in...in my life that you don't understand.''

''*I* have complications, too.'' Then he threw his hands up. ''My dad and his stinking millions aren't complications? *Everybody* has complications.''

Not all complications are equal, she thought. *You didn't bring yours on yourself.* I did.

''And it doesn't get much more complicated than being a single father—''

Kitt shot him an intense look. ''Tanni is a *blessing*.''

He gave his head a shake, as if she'd misunderstood. ''Of course she is. I meant—I know you'll need time to adjust to her. And what about the complication of two more years of poverty while I finish my education without my father's backing—''

''Without his backing?''

He ran a hand over his face and sighed as if resigning himself to telling her something he'd rather not. ''I tested his LinkServe offer, Kitt, like you suggested. I told him I'd take LinkServe as a gift, but that as soon as I had control I would sell off the stock and use the money to build a life of my own, as a journalist, with Tanni under my own roof.''

Kitt stared at him, openmouthed, and Mark gave her a sardonic smile.

''Let's just say he didn't take that real well,'' he continued, shaking his head. ''Boy, oh boy, he did not take that well at all. It's like I told you," he finished sadly. "LinkServe is just a tool my father uses to keep me under his thumb."

Kitt started to touch his shoulder, stopped herself. "You mean he just cut off all your funds?"

He looked away, "I have some Masters Multimedia stock that's not restricted. I can sell it to anybody I want. And I still have my scholarships." Then he shot her a glance, his eyes full of determination. "And my stringing pays pretty well, even if it isn't steady. And Carly wants to come back to Oklahoma with me—she loves it there, or she loves the cowboys, I don't know which." He inclined his head again and looked up into her downcast face.

She felt tears building. Great grieving tears for the man she was losing, the kind of man who had the integrity to walk away from millions of dollars rather than let another own his soul.

"Don't you see?" he went on. "We can make it because we have *love,* the real kind." He scooped a tear from her jaw with one finger. "Kitt, this showdown with my dad was bound to happen sooner or later." His voice was normal now. "And besides, LinkServe or not, someday I'm going to be one rich son of a bitch. You know I am." He gave her a shaky grin.

Oh, more than his tears, more than anything he had said, it was that sweet grin that broke her heart.

He was so sure everything would work out. Life would be good. And maybe it would…but not with her.

She turned her face away. "No. You don't understand. It can never work," she whispered. She should tell him. *Now,* her conscience urged. But she had kept her sad secret all these years, and keeping it locked away one more time came all too easily. How could she ever make him understand her decision when his own choice had been so different? How could she spend the rest of her life raising Tanni, missing her own child every time she looked at his? No. Despite everything he had said, her original decision was firm. She started backing toward the door, putting necessary distance between them.

His face became drawn, denial in his eyes. "Kitt. No," he whispered. He seemed frozen, unable to reach out to stop her as she retreated into the house. She heard him pleading as she turned inside, "Don't do this. Please."

She closed the door behind her and leaned weakly against it. From the moment she'd given up her baby, somewhere in her heart she had always known there would be a price to pay. She just hadn't known that price would be so high.

CHAPTER FOURTEEN

MARK DIDN'T GIVE UP immediately. He called several times, and each time Kitt was adamant about not seeing him. For the next few weeks she didn't go to the congressman's office, and since Mark's work at the CRM was done, they didn't run into each other. Finally, he left Washington, and Kitt succeeded in burying herself in her work. But it was a shaky, grim process.

All through late summer and early fall, she doggedly wrote briefs, constructed arguments, crafted the legislation. She organized volunteers, counted votes, scrounged funds. But the very work that she had once found so fulfilling seemed hollow now, utterly draining.

Even on the day when the big windfall came, she felt as if part of her was only going through the motions.

Reverend Dale showed up at the CRM offices bright and early. "This is most odd—" he held out an envelope "—but someone contacted the church yesterday on behalf of a private trust."

Kitt drew out a cashier's check made out to the Coalition for Media Responsibility, drawn on the Commonwealth Bank of San Francisco for one hundred thousand dollars.

Kitt stared at the sum. "But who—"

"I don't know. I made the courier wait while I called the bank. They said they couldn't advise us about anything but the trust number—871. The donor wants to remain anonymous. I was told to sign for the check and deliver it here."

"Amazing," Kitt breathed, and sank into a chair.

Reverend Dale did the same. "I'll say." He nodded his head. "It's the answer to our prayers."

Kitt only stared at the check. *Mark.* This was his way of getting rid of his unrestricted stock. Another way to rebel against his father—furthering the coalition's goals. She sighed, and the reverend looked puzzled at her less-than-joyous reaction. "At least this will let us do our direct mailing before the elections. If enough people contact their representatives, the bill might pass."

"And with the direct mailing—" the reverend clasped his hands "—you can raise even more funds!"

Kitt did smile then, for the reverend's benefit, and for all those who had worked so hard to see this thing through.

She made up her mind not to waste a dime of

Mark's money, and pushed herself harder than ever. And while she worked, she tried to be the old Kitt, the clever, self-assured, highly principled Kitt.

But there were cracks in this facade. More than once, she was late for a meeting or an appointment. Her nails became chipped and chewed instead of perfectly manicured. She stopped socializing. Even Jeff couldn't persuade her to indulge in an evening out.

When word reached the coalition offices that Congress had narrowly passed the hard-fought media bill, Kitt did manage a spirited "Hot dang!" for the benefit of the staff. And she was careful not to let them see the tears that came later, after Congressman Wilkens had called her to offer his personal congratulations.

"Kitt, my girl," Wilkens had boomed over the speakerphone around which the volunteers had huddled, sharing the kudos. "I expect you and your little coalition bunch are mighty pleased."

Kitt was leaning over the speaker, a smile set on her face for the sake of the volunteers. "Thank you for your vote of support, sir," she answered sincerely.

"Well, now, how could I do otherwise?" the congressman protested. "What with young Masters's glowing report about the coalition's research, about how—what'd he write?—*compelling* it was and all.

If Marcus Masters's own son saw the benefits in the legislation, how could I do anything but support it?''

The volunteers were dancing jigs and silently high-fiving each other. They didn't notice—at least she hoped they didn't notice—the tears that suddenly stung at her eyes.

Half an hour later, safely locked in the small bathroom connected to her office, she allowed the tears to fall. Mark, she thought as she dabbed at her overflowing eyes with a paper towel, how like him to be fair, to report the truth. As she examined her wretched reflection in the dim little mirror, she wondered if she would ever get over the loss of this man. She released a shaky sigh, dampened the paper towel, pushed aside her bangs and blotted her face. When she was finished she stared into her own sad green eyes and mumbled, "Woman, you deserve to feel empty."

As THE WEEKS PASSED, she worried that her emptiness was not just the result of losing Mark, that it was more pernicious, a re-exposure of older, deeper wounds.

The old dream returned, leaving its residue of gray fear.

Several more weeks passed before she stopped her irrational checking and rechecking of the answering machine first thing upon her arrival home in the evenings. Standing over the machine, cupping it between her palms as if it were Mark's face, listening for the sound of his deep voice, the sound that was not there.

She scrolled down her e-mail, both at the office and at home, so often that she thought she'd go blind. But what was she looking for? she asked herself. He wouldn't contact her. Mark didn't play games.

By the time the weather had turned cool, she had also stopped checking her mailbox for letters. There were none, would be none. Lauren unobtrusively brought in the mail after that, leaving Kitt's pile—with no word from Mark—resting mutely on the hall table.

This, Kitt told herself miserably, was what she had wanted, wasn't it? To let him go.

But even when these compulsions were under control, Kitt managed to punish herself in other ways. She could not pass a newsstand without checking the *Dallas Morning News* for his byline, and when she found it, she bought the paper and spirited it away to some quiet spot where she read and reread every word of his latest article. She clipped each one, folding it into an accordion file she kept upstairs in her bedroom. Sometimes late at night she leafed through the clips, reading his words again, imagining what he had been doing, how he had done the research, whom he had been with. One day there was an article about the Coalition for Responsible Media.

Kitt was standing at a newsstand in Union Station, getting ready to catch the Metro back to Alexandria, when she opened the features section and saw a photo of herself, making that speech at the rally. Her knees went weak and she had to steady herself, gripping the Metro pylon. That was the day everything had fallen apart for her, the day she let him go. She found a bench and read the article through tears. Unbiased? Oh my, yes. He must have agonized over every word.

A week later, on a long, lonely Sunday afternoon, she found herself back at Dumbarton Oaks. She spent the entire afternoon wandering around, watching small yellow leaves flutter to the ground, listening to the wind sigh sadly among the dying flowers. She sat on a dry grassy hillock until the shadow of the old Bliss mansion covered her, until a guard had warily approached her and told her that the garden was closing now and she must leave.

She visited Murphy's, too, one night. Alone. Asked herself why, why as she listened to the singer's plaintive rendition of "The Rising of the Moon." Looked for what seemed hours toward the grimy pay phone at the back, thinking to call Oklahoma. Just call. Hi. I'm here at Murphy's, tossing down my third Harp. Listen. "The Rising of the Moon." *Our* song. Remember? Oh, my love, do you remember? Say you remember me.

She had fled the place in tears when the band struck up "The Minstrel Boy."

Of course, she did not call him on that night, nor on any night, no matter how fierce her yearnings. How could she do such a thing? Call him? After she had hurt him like that? And what would she say? *I know it was terrible what I did to you, but you see, you don't know the worst part. I'm a coward. Selfish. The absolute opposite of you.*

THE CHRISTMAS SEASON came, and a card with the return address of Miss Tanni Masters arrived. Carly must have addressed it for Tanni.

"Bless you, Carly," Kitt whispered as she lifted the envelope from the stack on the hall table. She pressed it against her breastbone then carried it around with her, but did not open it, all that evening. She ate a hearty dinner for once, soaked in a relaxing hot bath and then took the cherished letter with her to bed, hoping that it contained word of, or even, God please be so kind, word *from* Mark.

She propped herself up on three pillows, opened the envelope carefully with her silver letter opener and slowly withdrew the contents: a Christmas card, a two-page letter, a drawing on wide-ruled paper. She unfolded the drawing first.

A stout Santa was cramming himself down the chimney of an apartment building that resembled the

stark student housing that Kitt remembered from
O.U. Happy flowers bloomed from a bank of pale
blue snow, and out of the one lopsided window the
oversize face of a little girl smiled out, complete with
curly eyelashes.

Kitt raised the drawing to her lips and kissed it.
The smell of crayon instantly brought tears to her
eyes. Little Tanni. Be happy, sweetheart, she thought
as the tears spilled over. Santa will come to you,
wherever you are. Your daddy will see to that. She
thought of her own baby. What did his drawings look
like?

Her hands shook as she unfolded the letter, written
in purple ink in Carly's block-style penmanship:

Dear Kitt, Hi!

The *Hi* had a heart in place of the dot on the *i*.

Mark said you would not want us to write to
you, so I haven't. Hope that's okay. But Tanni
wouldn't stop bugging me until I sent you her
Christmas drawing. Sorry. You know how kids
are. Anyway, we are doing fine, even if we do
live in kind of a dump. I have a really neat job
at a really neat place—

Kitt smiled. Was there no other adjective besides
neat in the Masters lexicon?

—called The Lovelight. It's a vegetarian restaurant, so I get free food, and the people I work with are nice. I am taking good care of Tanni, taking her to church, meeting lots of neat guys and tolerating my grumpy brother as well as anyone can. We are going to Daddy's house in Carmel for Christmas, how about you? Tanni wants me to write a page from her and then I gotta go.

Love ya,
Carly

Kitt had caught her breath at the word *Mark* and again at the part about the grumpy brother. She read the letter twice, assigning all kinds of meanings to Carly's two references to him. How dare he tell Tanni and Carly she wouldn't want to hear from them! But perhaps he was only protecting them. Kitt couldn't blame him. He was the kind of man who would want to shield his daughter and younger sister from a person who might cause them pain.

As for the grumpy-brother part, she reread it feeling strangely exhilarated. Was she truly so base? Didn't she want the poor man to be happy without her? Of course she did. But then she read the passage again, and her heart beat faster. He was grumpy! Maybe he missed her as much as she missed him. He was grumpy!

She reread the last sentence of the letter. They were going back to California for Christmas. Perhaps Mark's father was softening up, or perhaps they merely had no place else to go.

She hadn't even considered her own Christmas plans yet, preferring not to think beyond each day, except where it concerned her work. Recently, her dad's long-distance calls, always budgeted, had become frequent and protracted, for him. His voice had even begun to carry a note of concern. "Everything going okay, hon?" He'd put her brothers and their kids on the line if they were handy, stretching out conversations when there was nothing much to say. She knew he sensed something was wrong. She should go back to Oklahoma for Christmas in order to reassure her family that everything was okay with her. She could at least do that much right.

She refolded Carly's letter, then opened the second page, Tanni's message written in Carly's hand.

The few words from the innocent child pierced Kitt like a sword. She pressed the paper to her breastbone again and bit her lip.

After a while she put the card and its attachments back in the envelope, then carefully tucked the packet under her pillow. She put her head on the pillow and slid her palm over the envelope, over the drawing of Santa inside, over the smiling self-portrait of the little child she'd grown so fond of. The little girl who was the exact age of the child she had given up. *Protect Tanni,* she prayed as she drifted into a sorrowing sleep. *Make Tanni happy.* And as always, she prayed, *Protect my baby, too.*

AFTER THE CARD CAME, Lauren and Paige became more worried about Kitt. She was working hard and accomplishing more than ever, but there were unmistakable signs that Kitt was falling apart. For months there hadn't been one flash, not even a spark, of the famous Kitt Stevens temper. But, even more worrisome, was Kitt's silence.

"It doesn't take a panel of psychiatrists to figure out what's wrong," Paige told Lauren one night when Kitt begged off trio practice again.

"Yeah," Lauren agreed as they set up the music stand and laid out the music. "The way she keeps rereading that letter and that card." Lauren had seen the return address the day it arrived. She shook her head sadly. "She really misses them."

"Who'da thought she and Mark were that serious?" Paige said.

"Anybody who'd ever seen them kissing."

After Kitt declined their invitation to go on the Scottish Christmas Walk, the two younger women worried aloud as they walked the few blocks home through a fresh snow. "I can't believe Kitt didn't come with us tonight," Paige brought up the subject.

"When is she gonna snap out of it? Maybe we shouldn't have let her brood for so long."

"It's hard to know what to do," Lauren agreed. She jammed her gloved hands in her pockets as they waited at a crosswalk.

"She's a mess. She's even losing weight." Paige sighed and repeated her refrain, "Who would have imagined they were that serious?"

Lauren pulled her hood tighter and fidgeted against the cold. "Kitt usually tosses men off like last year's old sweater. But Mark Masters was different."

"You can say that again. I'd be depressed, too, if I'd lost that hunk!" Paige's breath puffed in a white cloud in front of her. "We've got to do something. Or Kitt's gonna shrivel up and die. One of us should talk to her."

"Yeah, *one of us* should." Lauren glanced up at Paige, and was not at all surprised to see an expectant raised eyebrow. "I suppose you mean me."

"It falls under the category of touchy-feely, doesn't it?"

As they crossed the street in front of their town house, Paige and Lauren saw Kitt's profile through the fogged panes of the drawing-room window. She was sitting at her little rolltop computer desk. "Right now would be a good time," Paige urged.

"There is never going to be a good time for this,"

Lauren said, not at all certain how to approach her mission.

They unlocked the door, and Paige disappeared down the narrow hall toward the kitchen like a darting gazelle. "I'll make hot chocolate," she called out. Lauren grimaced at Paige's retreating back, then took her time stamping the snow off her boots on the small rug in the foyer. She stood in the doorway of the dimly lit drawing room, looking at Kitt's profile illuminated by the monitor. Kitt looked so sad.

"Kitt?" Lauren ventured softy. Kitt leaned toward the screen, working the mouse.

When Lauren didn't move, Kitt said, "How was the tour?" sounding stuffy-headed. Had she been crying again?

"Oh, great! Traditional music, light refreshments, enough historical facts to bore even you. And the snow…" Lauren hesitated. "I wish you'd gone with us."

Kitt blinked at the screen.

Lauren pulled a small bentwood chair close to the desk and sat down. "Kitt, don't you think you should talk to someone about this?"

"Talk to someone?" Kitt said, gripping the mouse. Her other hand, Lauren noticed, covered a piece of paper in her lap.

Lauren felt a pang of dread and leaned in closer. "Mark's gone. You can't keep eating your heart out about it. You're losing weight. You'll make yourself ill.''

Kitt shook her head. ''You don't understand.''

Lauren bit her lip, unsure how to proceed, then said, ''What have you got there?''

Kitt gazed down at the paper and replied softly, ''A note…from Tanni.''

Lauren kept her voice equally soft. ''Is that the other part of it? You miss Tanni, too?''

Kitt shook her head again, then corrected herself, and nodded. ''Well, yes, I do miss Tanni. I don't know how I could have gotten attached so quickly—'' Kitt stopped. She *did* know how, and that was the trouble. Somehow Tanni had come to stand for her own child. ''But Tanni's not the whole problem, either.''

''Kitt, whatever is eating you, maybe I can hel—''

''No,'' Kitt interrupted her. ''No one can help me. What I've done—'' She shook her head fiercely. ''Is done.''

''It can't be that bad,'' Lauren argued softly.

''You don't know what you're talking about!'' Suddenly Kitt jumped up and ran from the room.

''Kitt!'' Lauren called after her, but the only reply she heard was the front door slamming.

The paper Kitt had clutched in her lap had fallen onto the floor at Lauren's feet. She stared at the little white square, then bent to pick it up. The note was

so brief, she'd read the whole thing before she realized perhaps she shouldn't have:

Dear Miss Kitt,
    We're going to Grandpa's so I can ride horses
and I made a birthday present to Baby Jesus.
It's a special prayer for my mommy.

Love,
Tanni

CHAPTER FIFTEEN

KITT DIDN'T FEEL the snowflakes hitting her cheeks, the gusts of wind at her back or the wetness soaking into her tennis shoes. She didn't hear the whoosh of tires in the slush, the occasional honking horns or the carolers at the corner of King and Fairfax.

She didn't notice the quaint Christmas decorations on the rows of town houses, the circles of warmth the streetlights made in the dark snowy air or the other pedestrians' holiday smiles as she hurried past them on the sidewalks.

The one thing that finally caught Kitt's attention was a figurine of the baby Jesus in a store window. Oh yes, she saw that baby.

It stopped her in her tracks in front of the tiny shop on Union Street. The infant statue lay at the center of a group of foot-high ceramic figurines depicting the Nativity with lifelike beauty.

Kitt stared into the window, seeing nothing but that scene. Joseph's manly protective stance. Mary's shining countenance. The babe in the manger. Safe with his mother.

She remembered the awesome responsibility she'd felt as a third-grader playing the role of Mary in the Christmas play. She was so scared when she peeked out the curtain at the audience of parents and teachers. But then she'd found her mother's smiling face. She'd gone onstage and kept her own little face poised just so. Her skinny legs had trembled with the effort of kneeling up straight for so long, but she'd done her role. She'd taken care of the baby. And her mother had been so proud of her.

But shortly after that, her mother was gone. Gone forever. Kitt closed her eyes and put her forehead against the window of the shop. The cold glass braced her briefly. Muffled voices on the other side of the glass startled her and she jerked back. Her breath had formed a foggy oval on the glass. Inside the cramped display window, a chubby young woman bumped around, talking over her shoulder to a customer standing nearby. The salesgirl gave Kitt a wary glance and Kitt caught her own reflection in the glass; she looked disheveled, scary. Kitt backed up a foot, but didn't move on down the sidewalk.

A middle-aged couple stopped at the shop to inspect the wares. They took each other's hands and stood near Kitt, watching the activity inside the window.

The salesgirl first handed the customer the statue of Mary, then the one of Joseph, then she picked up the one of Baby Jesus and climbed awkwardly out of the window. Just as she was bringing her hind foot over the low rail, she lost her balance and the baby Jesus slipped. "Be careful!" Kitt yelled against the glass, and the older couple turned to her. The young woman batted the figure like a fumbled football for one millisecond before it crashed to the floor.

"Oops!" The middle-aged man smiled.

"Oh God!" Kitt cried, and covered her mouth as she backed away from the window.

"Are you okay, hon?" the middle-aged lady asked.

Kitt could only shake her head as she continued to back away. No, she was definitely not okay. She turned and hurried down the sidewalk.

She felt as if she couldn't breathe as she rushed along. She had to do something, anything, to relieve this emptiness. She tried to get her bearings. How far was she from Murphy's? Maybe a Harp would help.

She stopped beneath a streetlight, then stumbled over to lean against a low brick wall and catch her breath. The snow had soaked her hair completely, and she pushed her limp bangs out of her eyes, drew in a gigantic breath. Why had she let that incident upset her so?

"Help me," she whispered, and turned her face up to the falling snow. She watched the flakes, back-lit by a street lamp, and was mesmerized for a moment by their endless, varied cascade. They were like tiny, whirling, living things. She blinked as they stuck to her lashes and her vision blurred with tears.

She remembered something her third-grade teacher, Sister Angelica, had said, "Snowflakes are like bits of peace sent down from heaven." Kitt had loved Sister Angelica so much. The sister had provided Kitt's only warmth the year her mother died. The next year, Kitt had gone to the public school, and she had never seen Sister again.

Third grade, when everything was so simple. If it were only that simple now. If she could only *do* something, maybe she would feel better. She pushed herself off the wall and wandered down the sidewalk. When she rounded the corner, the white lights decorating the evergreens in front of old St. Mary's Church glowed in the darkness. Kitt stared at the lofty high-spired building, remembering how she had gone to church regularly with her mother as a small child. But when her father had pulled her out of her small parochial school, the ties with her mother's religion had been broken. Only later, in high school, did Kitt return to her mother's ways, and then she worshiped at the big Baptist church in town where all the other teens went. This old colonial-style structure bore no resemblance to either of the churches she had attended back in Cherokee, but Kitt was drawn inside.

Her wet tennis shoes squeaked on the plank-wood floor, and the vestibule, while open, seemed awfully dark. The only illumination came from inside the church proper—soft altar lights and flickering red votive candles off to one side. A huge Advent wreath, its candles cold, was the only sign that it was the Christmas season. Catholics don't decorate until the Eve, Kitt recalled.

Her eyes flicked to an empty mock-up of a stable and manger; no baby there yet. The austerity of the purple-draped church comforted Kitt, matched her mood.

The smell of old wood, fresh wax and lingering incense mingled in the darkness, imparting a fleeting moment of nostalgia, which swiftly transposed itself into guilt and doubt. She had an abrupt photo-flash memory of coming with her mother one time during Lent. She saw her mother's clasped hands, furrowed brow, eyes squeezed shut, and it occurred to Kitt that her mother must have already known she had cancer. Perhaps her mother had thought her faith would save her, and perhaps that explained her father's rejection of the Church after his wife died. But so many things had changed after her mother died, and it was all so long ago. Suddenly Kitt thought, what am I doing here?

Getting all sentimental about Christmas and Sister Angelica and her mother wouldn't help her get over

Mark. She had made her choices, and she'd have to live with those choices—all of them. She rubbed her forehead. Something about being in this old church made her jittery. She set her jaw, rounded the baptismal font, headed for the door.

In the vestibule, she almost collided with a tiny bird of a woman in a flaming orange jogging suit.

"Oh! Excuse me!" Kitt said. The woman had seemed to materialize out of the dark!

"Did I startle you?" an incongruously deep voice asked. "It's these shoes, I guess. Brand-new and dangerously quiet." The woman turned up one foot so that Kitt could inspect a Nike Air Supreme, glowing ghostly white in the dark.

"Uh, that's okay," Kitt said, and stepped around.

"Were you wanting to go to confession?" The woman's low, smooth voice halted Kitt as it resonated in the silent church.

Kitt turned. "Confession?"

The woman nodded and her fluffy salt-and-pepper hair bobbed. She raised a delicate hand. "I'm sorry. Father Tom is ill. That's why I'm here," she said. "Oh... Oh, not to hear confession." The woman covered her mouth and behind her dated bifocals her hazel eyes glinted as if that were a great joke. "Just to tell any people that there'll be no confessions tonight. I'm sorry."

"I see. Well, thank you very much," Kitt turned to leave.

"This isn't an emergency, is it?" the woman said to Kitt's back. That voice, so incredibly rich, seemed to vibrate through Kitt's bones.

Again, Kitt stopped in her tracks. What a weird question. Was there such a thing as a spiritual emergency? She turned.

The woman smiled. "I mean, if something is wrong, you could talk to me, and maybe I could help." She studied Kitt's appearance sympathetically, and Kitt imagined she did look strange, inappropriately dressed for the weather, straggle-haired from the wet snow. "We are always here to help."

"We?" Kitt hesitated, deciding.

"Yes. I work here. I'm Sister Claire." The woman extended her slender hand. "And you are?"

Kitt took the hand; it was as soft as velvet around Kitt's thin cold fingers. "Kitt—" Kitt hesitated at giving her full name. She supposed this petite lady, with her casually styled, graying hair, her glittering eyes and—Kitt's glance flicked downward—that huge Southwestern-style cross hanging over her bosom, *could* be a nun. But she was certainly unlike any nun Kitt had ever encountered back in her parochial-school days. She was certainly no Sister Angelica.

The sister smiled again. "Well, Kitt, if you need to talk—" she spread her arms "—here I am."

Kitt felt strangely rooted to the floor. Part of her wanted to flee, to run, but part of her felt drawn to the short figure dressed in emergency orange. Something about her manner was so non-threatening, so inviting.

"Do you want to sit down?" the sister asked.

Kitt nodded and the nun walked to a back pew where Kitt slowly sank to the seat as if pulled by magnetic force.

"What is bothering you?" The sister motioned Kitt over and perched on the edge of the pew. "What can I help you with?" the nun repeated.

And then, shocking even herself, Kitt blurted out, "I gave my child away." Just like that.

The sister frowned and clasped her hands over her knees. "You gave your child away?"

"Yes. I...I gave my baby up for adoption."

"Oh. I see. That is a heartbreaker."

Kitt nodded. For that was it, exactly. Her heart was broken. Broken by guilt and loss. But there was more. There was fear, too. And the fear was the thing. The perpetual, nagging fear that maybe her child was not all right. Because of her own selfish, stubborn decision, she would never know.

"The worst part of it is..." Kitt glanced up at the silent statues witnessing her words from their dark alcoves, then she hurried to voice what she had always kept secret, before she lost her nerve. "I keep thinking, what if my child—my son—what if he isn't all right?"

"You don't know where he is? You don't know who the parents are?"

Kitt shook her head. "I insisted on a closed adoption. I was angry at the father. He refused to marry me, rejected me, rejected the baby. He even suggested an abortion. I couldn't do that, but I wanted to remain totally anonymous, to go back to my life as if none of it had ever happened. I...you see, I was very hurt, and I thought I could put it all behind me that way. But something has happened that made me see that it isn't behind me at all." Tears stung at Kitt's eyes as, for the first time ever, she admitted all of this out loud.

Sister Claire flicked her thumb nails nervously against each other as if she was trying to decide what to say.

"Until this moment, I've never talked about my baby to anyone except some friends in Tulsa who helped me at the time, and the counselor at the birth center."

"Not your family?"

Kitt shook her head. "I'm not close to my family. My mother died when I was eight and my father and my brothers...they're farmers. They...they live in their own world. It's not my world. I was in law school when I got pregnant, far from home. I...I made up lies. The friends in Tulsa covered for me."

The sister drew in a huge breath. "I see. But even though you kept the pregnancy a secret, it wasn't wrong to give your baby up for adoption. If you thought he would have a better life, loving parents."

"It wasn't that noble a decision..." Kitt broke off as tears choked her. "And now, I keep having nightmares. Or a nightmare, I should say. The same one. About a baby—" sudden tears choked Kitt "—about a baby floating away...into nothingness. But in my heart, it's like he's always out there. A little ghost." Kitt drew a great shuddering breath and Sister Claire squeezed her arm sympathetically.

"I guess I just *can't* get past it." Kitt looked directly into Sister Claire's eyes, having come at last to this simple truth.

Sister met Kitt's gaze with one of acceptance. She produced a Kleenex from her pocket and handed it to Kitt.

"And then, tonight, I saw a figurine of Baby Jesus—" At this a tortured sob escaped Kitt's throat, echoing in the dark, empty church. Kitt drew a deep breath, dabbed at her eyes and went on.

"And it reminded me of being in a play when I was little, in third grade, the same year my mother died...but all of a sudden the woman in the shop dropped the statue and broke it, and I thought I'd start screaming right there on the street. I realized I didn't think I could be a mother—that's why I gave my baby away. Not because I needed to finish law school, not because I was poor, not because the father had abandoned me. Deep down, I was just plain afraid to be a mother. And I still am. That's why I broke up with Mark. Oh, I don't know why I'm telling you all of this. It's all mixed up.''

''Mark?''

Kitt turned and the nun's bright eyes seemed to probe the pain in Kitt's. Kitt looked away again, fixing her gaze on the red votives at the front of the church. The real problem was Mark, of course, Mark and Tanni.

''Yes. I met someone and he has a little girl the same age as my baby. I feel like I'm abandoning my child all over again, like I'm being disloyal or something.'' Kitt squeezed her eyes shut, but the soft lights of the votives burned on in her vision. ''The baby was so small,'' she finished in a hurt voice, her hands fluttering near her heart. ''I told you, it's all mixed up.''

Sister Claire patted Kitt's arm. ''It sounds to me like you are having trouble letting go of the past. But maybe over time I can help you. I have helped others in similar situations.''

Over time? Kitt didn't want to get involved in any

long-term way. It was a mistake—coming in here.
What had ever possessed her? Kitt didn't have much
hope that time would help anyway—she had been at
this crossroads with her feelings before. "I probably
shouldn't have come here," she said. "I'm sorry I
bothered you." She was already standing, already
backing out of the pew.

"You didn't bother me," Sister said quietly. "I
am here to help people."

"I do sincerely thank you for listening...and for
caring," Kitt added more softly, "but I really think
I'll just have to work this out on my own. It's my
burden."

The sister searched Kitt's eyes briefly once more,
then answered reluctantly. "All right. But remember,
if you need me, I am always here."

Kitt only nodded.

"Go in peace," the sister said softly as Kitt turned
away.

Kitt blindly edged down the pew to the side aisle.
When she glanced back once, she saw the nun lowering her small frame onto the kneeler and pressing
her forehead to folded hands.

Go in peace echoed in Kitt's mind. But Kitt felt
no peace, no peace at all, as she fled the dark church
and went back out into the cold winter night.

CHAPTER SIXTEEN

KITT SPENT more than she should have on extravagant Christmas gifts and flew back to Oklahoma for the holidays.

Throughout that Christmas visit, first with her friends in Tulsa and then at her father's farm near Cherokee, she tried to forget, tried to outrun her summer love and the bleak season that had followed it. She tried to let go of the past, as the sister had said.

But little things would cause memories and tears to well up: the Christmas program in which her niece played the Virgin Mary; a chance encounter in the local Wal-Mart where an old high-school pal showed off pictures of four-year-old twins.

Her family was mystified by her weepy, distracted behavior. Kitt had always been the strong, wisecracking girl who gave her brothers back whatever they dished out.

Her dad, never one for talking much, asked her to sit down one evening before they left for a neighbor's annual open house.

They took their seats at the dinette set in the

kitchen, and her father folded his big, leathery hands tightly on the worn Formica tabletop. As she stared at those work-roughened hands, at the scrunched sleeves of his gray Sunday suit, at that same Santa tie he'd worn to the Sadlers' open house every year, Kitt's melancholy grew deeper somehow.

"Kitt, I'm worried about you," he started. "I can't understand why you're so unhappy. Especially it being Christmastime, and all." He added this last in a slightly accusatory tone, as if she were intentionally spoiling the holiday season.

Her father's way—stiff-upper-lip, down-to-earth, back-to-work—had been his defense ever since her mother's death. And Kitt suddenly realized that she had absorbed those exact defenses, even using them to tough out the birth of her own child.

"If something bad has happened to you," he said in his straightforward way, "I'd like to know about it."

The thought that she had never been able to tell her father about anything, good or bad, caused Kitt's throat to close up, and when she didn't speak, he responded by checking his watch, signaling that this talk couldn't drag on too long. "You aren't sick or something, are you?" he prompted.

"No. I've had some...some professional setbacks, that's all. Haven't performed up to par at work, stuff like that. I'm sorry, really I am, if I've been moody."

Kitt slipped a hand over his in apology, in placation. "Really, Dad. I'm sorry."

He patted her back, then drew his rough hand out, satisfied that he'd done his parental duty. "Well. Everyone has rough times, especially in a high-powered career like yours, I expect. The Sadlers will be looking for us."

Kitt nodded, letting him off the hook. Her father always found a way to convey the message that he didn't really want to be inconvenienced, that the seasons of farming could never be suspended. In the same way you didn't want to be inconvenienced? she accused herself. The same way you didn't want to interrupt law school? She rubbed her forehead.

"You know what?" Kitt pasted on a smile, then looked around her father's cramped, cluttered kitchen. "I think I'd rather stay home tonight. Do a little holiday baking and cleaning. Why don't you go on and have a good time at the Sadlers' without me?"

He'd left without a fuss, and in the days after that he didn't press her about her troubles. But the silence in the old farmhouse only increased her loneliness and pain, and finally she couldn't stand it any longer.

She called Mark, knowing his machine would pick up. He and Tanni and Carly were in Carmel, having Christmas with his father. It was merely the sound of his voice she sought, not actual contact.

"This is Mark Masters," the recording began. His voice, so deep, so clear and resonant, sent a tremor through her. She gripped the phone so hard that her knuckles blanched. "At the tone, please leave a message. Don't forget to leave your number, the date and time. I'll get back to you." *Beep.*

She dialed three more times and listened. Even delivering that straightforward message, his voice thrilled Kitt.

That night she barely slept.

WHEN WHAT PROMISED to be a long, gray Christmas Eve Sunday dawned, Kitt made her decision. This was *her* Christmas trip, after all, and all the usual holiday diversions weren't working anyway. She was going to celebrate Christmas her way.

She took a quick shower, skipped the makeup, pulled on an old sweater, jeans, boots, a faded jean jacket, and left her dad a reassuring note.

She stopped at the Wal-Mart in Enid to make her purchases, hit the drive-through at McDonald's for breakfast and ate as she drove. The greasy hash browns and rubbery eggs tasted delicious—she actually had an appetite for once. She supposed because she actually had a purpose for once.

As soon as she arrived in Norman, she found a phone book, looked up the address. Student housing, just as she'd guessed. She would find nothing but a drab apartment door in a giant complex where hundreds lived behind identical drab doors. But this would be *Mark's* door.

She wondered if it was foolish, leaving the glittery gift bags tied to the door handle. *Like it's not foolish to even be standing here,* she thought. But surely no one would steal the tiny bags at Christmastime. She smiled at the lopsided homemade wreath on the door. Carly.

She was tying the handles of the bags around the knob, when the door suddenly jerked open.

There he stood. Barefoot, shirtless, baggy sweatpants drooping well below his navel, staring at her as if she had just beamed down from Mars.

Kitt's heart stood still.

"Kitt," he said with a rush of air, as if someone had heaved a medicine ball into his middle. He raised one hand and laid it over his heart. With the other he raked back his wild dark hair.

The blood rushed to Kitt's head, then seemed to drain everywhere else at once, and she feared she might faint. He stood so close that she could smell him—a warm, sleepy, been-in-these-clothes-a-while fragrance that sent her senses reeling. "Mark!" she exhaled. The gift bags had been jerked from her hand when he opened the door and lay at their feet. "I was just dropping off Christmas gifts." She stooped to pick them up. "For the girls. I...I hope that's okay. I...I didn't expect to find anyone home."

"Oh?" He frowned and reached up and smoothed through his hair again. She focused her eyes back on the gift bags.

"Well, I, um, I thought you'd be in Carmel—" She caught herself, remembering that he'd told Carly not to write to her.

"No. Only the girls went. I had too much work to do." Then he seemed to realize he was barring the doorway. He backed up and held the door open. "It's cold out there. Would you like to come in? I mean, can you stay for a minute?"

Kitt felt rooted to the ground, her mind refusing to work, her glib lawyer's tongue struck mute.

"Kitt?" Mark said, taking her elbow lightly. "Come on in and warm up." Gently he urged her to move.

He steered her past the threshold and reached behind her to close the door.

The apartment was dim and quiet, with the drapes still drawn and a heater closet humming softly. Kitt could hear a clock or a timer over in the tiny kitchenette, ticking in the dark silence.

"Did I wake you up?" she asked, horrified to realize that she probably had. What time was it, anyway? She'd left Cherokee just after dawn.

"Wake me?" Mark said as he slipped around her

and switched on a cheap pole lamp by the couch. "No. No, I was getting up anyway. I've got a big article to write. Deadline's tonight." He crossed the room and switched on another tiny table lamp, then put a knee to the couch under the window and opened the drapes halfway.

The living room was microscopic, with a linoleum floor and garage-sale furnishings—and enough Christmas decorations to smother a small grade school. A real Christmas tree, scrawny and weighed down with decorations, twinkled in the corner. A short bar with three stools separated the kitchenette from the main room. Tanni's drawings plastered the refrigerator. The whole place was saturated with the homey smell of vegetarian cooking and a frequently used bread-making machine.

"Sit down." Mark gestured to the couch. "Would you like some coffee?" He dashed into the kitchenette before she answered, and started rinsing last night's old coffee and grounds down the drain.

"Okay," Kitt said uncertainly as she lowered herself to a hideous orange-and-brown flowered couch. How had she gotten herself into this?

"Excuse the mess. Carly would have a fit about it, but I've been working night and day since the girls left. Besides, I haven't had the heart to do much else. Christmas without Tanni is a bummer—don't you want to take off your jacket?—but I just couldn't make myself go to Carmel. I couldn't handle my dad. Things are still rocky between us. I think it's going to take him a while to get used to the fact that I'm not under his thumb anymore.''

He said all this over his shoulder as he filled the coffee machine, and Kitt sat there watching him, listening to him talk as if they were picking up a conversation they'd started yesterday. She watched the muscles in his back flex as he raised the pot to pour the water in the machine. Mechanically she slipped off her jean jacket. On the coffee table in front of her, his laptop screen glowed amidst a litter of papers and books.

''But I haven't changed my mind about LinkServe. I've never felt so free. I've even scraped together enough money to pay back the loan.''

The phone rang. He glanced over his shoulder. ''Ignore it. The machine's on.'' There was the familiar message, then a *beep*.

''Hey, bud.'' It was a young male voice. ''You told me to call and get you out of the rack. Something about a deadline.'' There was a deep chuckle and the machine clicked off.

Mark smiled. ''A true friend.'' He switched on the coffeemaker.

Kitt felt as if she were in a dreamworld. Mark was actually making coffee for her. She could take five steps across this little room and actually touch that beautiful bare back. "The loan?" she said, trying to keep the conversation going, to sound casual.

"Yeah." He turned to face her. "The loan for the money I paid Tiffany to have Tan—" He stopped abruptly. "Oh, yeah," he breathed. "We never got a chance to talk about that."

"Talk about what?" It seemed to Kitt that all she could manage to do was parrot his own words back to him.

"About how I got Tanni."

No, they *hadn't* talked about that, Kitt realized with a jolt. None of it. She wanted to tell him she knew something about Tanni's beginnings, from Carly at church. But might that create bad feelings between brother and sister? After all, even though Carly was young and naive, maybe Mark wouldn't appreciate her telling his story at church.

"Tell me about it," Kitt said, though she knew her heart might break, hearing him tell it.

He stepped into the living room, wiping his hands on a dish towel. "Well, I was never married for one thing. I guess that's the first thing I'd like you to know." He crossed the room and sat down on the couch beside her, but not too close. "I did offer to marry her. Tiffany, I mean. That was her name."

Kitt wondered how deeply he had been involved with this Tiffany. Enough to make love to her, obviously.

"Marriage wasn't what she wanted," Mark continued. "She was young. I don't blame her for any of it. She had scheduled an abortion, and I was going to go with her, but the closer the date got, the more…I don't know…the more panicky I felt."

Kitt felt weak. She closed her eyes, opened them again, looked at Mark. He was sitting forward on the couch, with his legs spread wide, an elbow propped on each knee, his clasped hands pressed to his forehead. "Finally I told my mother what was going on. She begged me not to allow Tiffany to go through with it. She said she'd raise the child.

"So I went to my dad and asked for enough money to convince Tiffany not to have the abortion." He heaved a huge sigh, lowered his hands and looked in Kitt's eyes. He smiled. "Twenty-five thousand dollars…that's how I got Tanni."

Kitt's heart beat in a crazy rhythm for an instant, then, in a voice so flat, so normal, she could hardly believe it was herself talking, she said, "I'd say you and Tanni are both very, very lucky."

Mark sighed again. Smiled again. "Yeah. We are. Well, *I* am. But sometimes, I gotta tell you—" he looked at a studio portrait of Tanni on the opposite wall and spread his large hand across his biceps "—sometimes I think Tanni got a raw deal. I mean, I try, but I'm…well—" he kept rubbing his muscle and Kitt wondered if she was staring "—I'm no substitute for a mother."

Depends on the mother, Kitt thought. What was she doing here? If she dared to look at him again she might cry. Then what? He'd wonder why. And could she tell him?

"And now, since Mom died, Tanni has even less security. Carly's great, but she can't do this forever." He sighed. "Sometimes I feel like I've made a mess of everyone's life."

He looked up and his voice brightened. "Tanni made those." He smiled at the cut-out angels pasted onto the ceiling, then sobered. "I'm really glad I got the chance to tell you all of this. I always wanted to..." His voice trailed off.

They fell into an uncomfortable silence during which Kitt still couldn't bring herself to look at him.

But she could feel him studying her anxiously, no doubt gauging her reaction to his story, and she wanted to reassure him, to tell him that, in fact, she loved him for what he had done, that she had always loved him, that she would always love him. But to tell him that, she'd have to tell him her story first. Either that, or build their relationship on a lie.

She closed her eyes, allowing her fear to win out again.

"Kitt, are you okay?" he said softly.

She opened her eyes, adopted a masking smile. "Yes. I'm just...is that coffee ready yet?"

"Oh, sure!" He jumped up and padded into the kitchen.

"So you brought Tanni and Carly Christmas presents?" he said as he filled the mugs. "That's nice. I guess Carly sent you a Christmas card or something, huh? That's how you knew about their trip to Carmel?"

"Yes," she admitted while she struggled to regain her equilibrium.

"Carly sends Christmas cards to all of humankind. It is her high, holy holiday." He raised a mug to the room. "Do you think there are enough decorations in here? Maybe we need a few more stars, or some more tinsel or something?"

Kitt had to smile, and then their eyes met. Mark grew solemn and heaved a huge sigh. "It's so good to see you," he said quietly.

Kitt could only stare. She felt her lips part, and pressed them back together. Then she felt the tears she'd been suppressing well up.

"No, Kitt. Don't." He abandoned the mugs and crossed the room to her in three steps, knelt on one knee before her, grabbed her shoulders. "Don't. Please. Don't cry."

She looked down at her hands clasped in her lap, and was horrified to see a huge tear plop onto her crossed thumbs. "I'm sorry," she whispered. "I shouldn't have come here."

"Don't say that." He pulled her to him, and the breath she'd been holding left her in a powerful rush at the contact with his chest, with his heart.

"I'm *glad* you're here," he said against her ear. "When I saw you standing in the doorway for one split second I thought I should be mad at you, the way you dumped me, but the truth is, I'm not. The truth is…" Without releasing her, he slipped up onto the couch beside her. From touching her only once, his male need was already obvious in the sweatpants, and to Kitt it only made him seem more honest, more vulnerable. I should stop this right now, she thought, but it was too late. He was already speaking the words she dreaded.

"The truth is, I still love you," he whispered. He tilted her chin up a fraction, looked in her eyes. "The truth is, I always will."

The story of our relationship, she thought as she closed her eyes and her tears overflowed. *Mark speaking out the very things that I am terrified to say.*

She felt him reading her face for a moment, then he scooped a tear off her cheek and said, "Kiss me," very softly. "Just once."

Then slowly he brought his mouth down on hers. Kitt didn't resist him.

Everything came rushing back in that first instant of contact, as if they had never been apart. He tasted exactly as she remembered: the wonderful taste of Mark. She could feel his heart pounding wildly in his bare chest. He groaned and forced the kiss deeper, and Kitt was lost. Lost to passion, lost to him.

He turned her, flattening her against the couch. She put a palm on his chest. He was so warm! "Mark," she whispered his name in awe, and he answered, "Kitt," reverently before he fastened his mouth on hers again with a fierceness that surpassed mere passion.

He slipped a hand under her sweater, under her sports bra, and cupped her fully in his warm palm. At the same time he kissed her neck—no, *devoured* it—and the rush of sensation that went through her was unlike any she had ever felt. For so long she had denied herself this. It seemed like a miracle, feeling this way again. She opened her eyes and saw the paper angels above them. And to Kitt, their crayon faces looked joyous.

The phone rang again and Kitt jerked, but Mark raised his mouth just long enough to murmur, "Ignore it." Then he plunged back in and continued where he had been.

After the familiar beep a female voice spoke. "Mark, I know it's Christmas Eve, but you're always wanting to work extra. Here's your chance. I need you today and tomorrow. Call me." *Beep*.

Suddenly something clicked with Kitt and she wrestled free. "You're working on Christmas Day?"

"Yeah, I've got another job at the local paper, but I've always got time for you." Mark leaned forward to kiss her again.

But Kitt turned her head. She had a question to ask—one that she already knew the answer to. "You're the name behind the secret trust, behind the hundred thousand dollars," she blurted.

Mark froze. He raised his head, and when he looked in her eyes, his were steely with resolve. "I'm through with Masters Multimedia."

"So it *was* the unrestricted stock," Kitt whispered.

"My last tie to Masters Multimedia."

"Were you simply using me to get back at your father, to punish him for taking LinkServe away?" She had to know.

"No! I believe in the coalition's goals, just like you do. My father is dead wrong about that legislation, and it's my right to oppose him. I made the donation anonymously because I didn't want you to think I was trying to buy you back or something."

"But you and Tanni need that money."

"No we don't. We're fine. Carly's fine. We've even got a stupid little dog who's fine. Why can't you accept the fact that I like living like a normal guy?''

''Mark. I'm...'' She stood. ''I'm sorry. You...'' Kitt backed away. Her heart was pounding in a sickening rhythm. ''I don't want to be between you and your father.'' She spun around wildly, trying to find her purse through sudden tears. ''It can't ever work out between us.''

He jumped up and made her face him, wouldn't let her twist away. ''Why not? I love *you!*''

''Don't say that!'' Kitt wrenched her shoulders from his grasp. ''You don't even *know* me!'' She found her purse and jacket. ''Coming here was a mistake!'' she said as she jerked the door open.

MARK STOOD in the open door and watched as Kitt ran down the sidewalk and rounded the empty pool in the apartment courtyard. He was torn, wanting to run after her, but he stopped himself. What good would it do? He'd been through all this in his mind a thousand times—all those times when he wouldn't let himself contact her. The woman either wanted him or she didn't. It was that simple.

He closed the door and lowered himself onto the couch, put his elbows on his knees and pressed his head into his palms, willing himself to feel anger at her so that he might not feel the other things: the pain and the despair. "Thanks, Kitt," he said bitterly. "Thanks a lot for coming by."

After a long time he noticed the gifts Kitt had brought, still sitting on the end table. He picked them up, looked down into the little sacks. Inside one was a pair of silver cross earrings, obviously for Carly—Tanni's ears weren't pierced. And in the second sack carefully nestled in a bed of pink angel hair was a miniature Nativity set. Numbly, he walked over and placed both gifts under the tree. They were, after all, meant for Tanni and Carly. Gifts from Miss Kitt.

CHAPTER SEVENTEEN

KITT'S FIRST WEEKS BACK in Washington were brutal. Snow and sleet lashed the town throughout January, and the streets took on a perpetually slushy, dank cast. No sun broke through the daily veil of clouds, allowing layers of ice to build up on the bare cherry trees and exposed monuments. Even the Tidal Basin—that rosy, steamy setting where Mark had first proposed lovemaking to Kitt—was frozen solid. This gloomy outer world matched Kitt's inner one perfectly.

Nights were the worst. She wanted desperately to know if Mark was confused or hurting after her foolish visit. She prayed that he wasn't, that he would forget about her. A new nightmare haunted her in which Mark sat with his back to her, his head in his palms. If only she'd had the strength to tell him the truth that morning in his apartment. She saw now how selfish she'd been to ever let him touch her again. But there was no going back, and the last thing she would do now was cause him more pain. She made up her mind this time; she would never see him again.

In her waking hours she resolutely applied her old coping mechanism—work, work and more work.

Her current goal was to solidify the considerable gains that the CRM had made since the bill had passed, and to make sure those legislators who had voted for it got rewarded at election time.

One hectic afternoon when she had already taped three radio actualities, and still had two congressional receptions to attend, Cecelia in the front office buzzed her desk. "Kitt, there's a young man out here to see you."

Kitt held her breath. *Young man?* Her mouth went dry. She felt her face heating up, and her heart proceeded to hammer so hard it felt as if it might bruise itself. But wouldn't Cecelia simply say "Mark" if it was Mark? Surely Cecelia remembered Mark. Everybody remembered Mark.

Kitt calmed herself, leaned over the intercom and said, "Who is it?"

Over the intercom, she heard Cecelia politely asking the visitor for a name. Then she heard a familiar male voice: "Tell her it's Danny Shipley."

Kitt stared at the phoneset, hoping she hadn't heard right. Danny Shipley? Here? Now? She had a sudden urge to laugh hysterically. Instead she forced herself to think. He was apparently standing right beside Cecelia's desk, and both would hear her response.

"Please ask him to take a seat and wait," was all she could think to say.

Danny's voice came back loud and clear, as if he were speaking directly above the intercom which he had apparently commandeered from the hapless Cecelia. "Kitt, it's *me,* Danny-boy!"

Kitt wanted to yell, *Danny-boy! Drop dead!* Instead, she leaned forward and, in a voice as cold as the ice sheeting the streets outside, she said, "Danny Shipley? Well, well. After all these years."

"How about that? Listen, we can't talk over this intercom. I'm coming on back." The intercom clicked off.

Kitt gripped the edge of her desk and gritted her teeth.

He burst through her office door with Cecelia in hot pursuit. The plump older lady froze when she saw the fiery malice in Kitt's eyes. Danny, suave and impeccable in a three-piece suit and black wool topcoat, only smiled broadly.

"It's all right, Cecelia," Kitt said quietly. "Please see that we're not disturbed."

Danny seemed oblivious to Kitt's enmity. While Cecelia backed out and quietly closed the door, he planted his hands on his hips as his eyes roved over the cramped room, the bare windows frosted with ice, the cheap dented desk. "Nice digs," he said, teasing. "Much better than that shabby corner office at the top of the Williams Center."

"You never saw my Tulsa office," Kitt informed him flatly.

"No, but I heard about it. I certainly heard. How could you leave all that elegance for this?" He spread his arms wide then, and answered his own question—wrongly—"The lure of Washington power, I guess." He smiled again. "Isn't this weird? Both of us working in D.C. now?"

Weird? Kitt thought. *It's positively vile.* "You're working in Washington?" she said.

He nodded. "Been here a whole week. I couldn't wait to get over here and see my little Kitten."

His little Kitten?

He bounded across the room, stepped behind her desk, invaded her space. "And she looks wonderful!" He swiveled her desk chair, grabbed her hands and yanked her to her feet.

Kitt did not extract herself from his grasp. She was too furious to. While he leaned back and ogled her figure, she stared at his high, handsome forehead, imagining how satisfying it would be to land an ax there.

"You're lookin' good, real good. A little on the thin side, as always."

You should have seen me when I was nine months pregnant. I wasn't so thin then.

He leaned forward, and she got a whiff of expensive cologne mingled with potent breath freshener.

"But you're still as beautiful as ever," he said, and stared into her eyes with his baby-blue ones, waiting for her reaction to his compliment.

Kitt glared a hole through him, her nostrils flaring with rage, and at last it seemed to dawn on him that her demeanor was less than friendly. "Kitten? Aren't you going to say anything?"

She wrenched her hands free. "Yes," she hissed. "I *am.* What the hell are you doing here?"

He recoiled as if she'd slapped him. "Hey! What's this? We haven't seen each other in almost five years and it's what the hell are you doing here?"

"You heard me. What are you doing here? Now?"

He backed up a step. "What do you mean, *now?*"

"I mean *now.* When I've made a life for myself, when I've finally put that fiasco we called a relationship behind me."

"Fiasco? *I* didn't think it was a fiasco. The only fiasco was that after you got pregnant, you kicked me out. No explanation. Not even a decent goodbye. If anybody should be pissed off here, babe, it should be me." He jabbed the front of his stiffly starched white shirt, then seemed to make a conscious effort to regain control. "That was a long time ago. We were just kids. We both made mistakes. I thought we could at least be friends now that we're working in the same town.''

''I don't need friends like you.''

''Kitt,'' he breathed as if genuinely shocked. ''Why are you treating me this way?''

She glared. ''Please leave.''

He frowned, obviously confused and deeply disturbed by her anger. ''Okay. If that's what you want,'' he said. ''If that's what you really want.'' But he made no move to go.

She stepped over to the frosted window and turned her back toward him. The sounds of the traffic below punctuated their silence. Finally he said, ''Here's my card,'' and she heard it snap onto her desk. Then she heard him walk out and close the door.

The minute he was gone, Kitt began to shake. She wrapped her arms around her middle and pressed her forehead against the cold glass in an effort to calm herself. The worst of it had not been how Danny looked—as polished and gorgeous as ever. Or how he acted—as arrogant and shallow as ever. The worst of it had been her realization that he was partly right. She had never told him that she'd given birth to their child. And then given that child away.

I SHOULD TELL HIM, she reminded herself for the hundredth time the next day as she dialed the number on the business card.

But what if Danny made a mess of things? Tried to contact the child? Kitt drew in a deep cleansing breath. Of course, he could never do that. After all, he'd been the one who'd opted for an abortion.

"Danny Shipley, please," she said when the receptionist at the law firm answered. "Tell him it's Kitt Stevens." She waited one full agonizing minute until he came on the line. When he said, "Kitt?" she said, "We need to talk," without preamble.

"Where?"

"You name it."

He chose the elegant Occidental Club adjacent to the Willard Hotel, and Kitt wished she hadn't given him the option. The Occidental, with its high-powered political clientele, seemed a little too public for the baring of her soul. But maybe the setting was a blessing. In this restrained environment with soft lighting, white tablecloths and elegantly dressed couples, she wouldn't be as likely to tear Danny's eyes out if he reacted badly again. Kitt asked the hostess for a secluded booth and didn't bother to counter Danny's wrongheaded smile about that.

They ordered drinks, and while they waited to be served, they made strained chitchat about the pictures of famous political leaders that covered the walls.

Danny talked about his work, but Kitt felt no desire to discuss hers.

As soon as the gin and tonics came, Kitt took a sip then said, "I'm sorry for the way I acted in my office yesterday, but I really don't want to see you while you're living up here. It's impossible. I'm sorry."

He ran a finger around the rim of his glass and gave her a little smirk. "Then what are we doing here?"

"We are making the fact that I don't want to see you crystal clear so you do not pop into my life unannounced ever again."

"You can't tell me a part of you wasn't secretly happy to see me."

"That is exactly what I am telling you, and I want you to stay away from me."

"Oh, Kitten, you don't mean that. We were so close once. The timing was wrong, that's all. But I always thought we kind of belonged together. Like two peas in a pod."

An unfortunate choice of metaphors, Kitt thought. Then she said very clearly, "No. We didn't belong together then." Before she could stop herself, she blurted out, "And we never will."

He blanched, but her long-buried anger was already boiling up, making her ruthless. "We were *not* close, Danny. We were physically involved, but we weren't close. Trust me on that. You kept secrets from me, and I kept secrets from you.''

His handsome face slowly changed from shocked white to angry red. "Secrets?"

Kitt decided to skip the pointless accusations about his philandering, to forgo presenting her irrefutable evidence of it, and just drop her bomb. "When you left Norman, did you suspect that I was still pregnant?"

He spilled his gin and tonic down his front, stared at her in horror for some seconds, then brushed off his tie with his napkin.

"You can't be serious," he breathed. "We had a deal. And now you're telling me you didn't get the abortion?" He stared at the tablecloth for a moment, then blinked.

"No, I didn't."

"Then what happened? You don't...you're not looking for child support or something, are you?"

It was very good indeed, Kitt decided, that they were smack in the middle of this fancy restaurant so that the urge to stab her salad fork into Danny's handsome Roman nose was inhibited by the civilized sound of live piano music and the sight of a waiter's tuxedoed back only a few yards from their table.

"Don't be ridiculous," she snapped. "I'm a lawyer. If that's what I wanted, I'd have had it long ago."

Danny's face flushed even redder. His eyes flicked sideways. Kitt knew that look. He was evaluating his options. He chose offense.

"The least you could have done was tell me," he accused.

"And what would you have done if I had?"

"Married you, of course!" He tossed his wadded napkin on the table as if some tough negotiation had ended his way. Kitt wanted to snatch up the cloth and throttle him with it.

"Married me? How convenient it must be to produce the noble response—in hindsight."

"Oh, and what was your noble response, sister? This lie? The last I heard, you had an abortion and I thought the whole mistake was behind us. But all the time, you were planning to keep the pregnancy."

"To keep the *baby*, Danny. It was a baby...a baby that you rejected."

"It was an accident!" He downed what was left of the gin and tonic. Then he studied her with new understanding in his eyes. "Okay. Where is this baby? I have a right to know."

For a heart-stopping moment Kitt considered his words, letting guilt convict her. "I suppose there is no one to blame but myself," she finally said. "I did make my choices unilaterally. In fact, I don't know why I'm telling you about it now, except to make you understand why I don't want to see you. There is too much sad history between us, at least in my mind."

"Yeah. I understand. I understand that you've been furious at me for years over something I didn't even know had happened. Thanks a lot, babe. Thanks for the honesty."

Honesty? Kitt thought. And suddenly Mark's face flashed through her mind. Secrets again. She and Mark had both kept secrets, but at least he had been planning to come clean about his, eventually. When was she going to learn her lesson and stop hiding things, stop trying to go it alone? When was she going to learn to tell the truth and let people have their own responses instead of always assuming she knew how they'd react? She hadn't given Mark a chance to accept her.

"So—" Danny was still talking "—you're all pissed off and guilty about a baby I didn't even know existed until this instant, and all this time you've neatly blamed the whole thing on me, when it was you who—"

"If we're going to be honest," Kitt interrupted, "let's be honest. I broke up with you because of Gina, and Shannon, and…" She had to make a conscious effort to keep her voice calm. "And wasn't there one with a weird name? Harolyn?"

For one instant he looked stunned, then he covered it. "Come on. We weren't committed or anything,

Kitt. The pregnancy was a simple accident. A screw-up. But now it's all my fault and I suppose you're scarred for life.''

Scarred for life? Kitt thought. *Scarred for life?* She imagined that's exactly what she was. With tears brimming in her eyes, she stood, glad that her decision four years ago would at least protect the child from this jerk. "That's about the size of it, Danny," she whispered. "Scarred for life." She strengthened her voice. "You can pay for the drinks. I'm getting my coat."

He grabbed her wrist. "You didn't tell me what happened to the baby."

The baby, not *my* baby, not *our* baby. "He's gone, Danny. He's with his family, where he belongs."

She turned on her heel and quickly wove her way through the tables, up the short flight of stairs, and out into the cold before her tears started to flow.

Let Danny Shipley think whatever he wanted about her. At least the baby would remain forever free of that selfish man.

CHAPTER EIGHTEEN

KITT COULD HEAR the voice even as she climbed the dark church steps. Husky. Flat. Slightly out of tune.

Sister Claire had told Kitt to meet her at the church at eight, she hadn't mentioned that she'd be singing. A gust of icy wind urged her to open the heavy door and slip inside to the warmth. She waited in the dark vestibule, listening.

For a moment she leaned into the sound of that off-key voice, drew strength from it. Then she crept quietly up the side aisle and stood beside a pew.

The white-haired organist stopped the music when he noticed Kitt. He looked up at Sister Claire, inclining his head toward the shadows.

"May we help you?" The nun's deep voice reached across the empty church like a wave of warm air.

Kitt stepped forward. "It's me, Sister. Kitt Stevens. I called you earlier."

"Of course." Sister Claire turned toward the organist. "We were finished here, weren't we, John?"

The elderly musician was already gathering his

music. When he passed Kitt on his way out, he gave her a kindly nod.

"Do you remember me?" she asked quietly as Sister Claire walked down the aisle. Tonight's jogging suit was a hideous shade of purple.

The nun extended her hand. "Yes. You are the one who—" she took Kitt's hand, squeezed it, covered it with her other warm one "—the one who is suffering from shadow grief…among other things."

"Shadow grief?" The phrase startled Kitt.

"Yes. A kind of emotional ache, a dullness. Not uncommon in your situation. You see, you are grieving for your lost baby. I've thought of you often, Kitt, since that night when we met. Would you like to go to my office where we can talk in comfort?" The sister already had a hand on Kitt's shoulder, guiding her.

Kitt nodded and allowed herself to be led toward the altar end of the church, through a creaking side door, then down a short hallway, ending up in a narrow office with a high ceiling buttressed by thick crown moldings. Sister Claire flicked on a soft lamp, then scooped up a stack of music books and a couple of stuffed teddy bears—one dressed like a traditional nun—making room for Kitt to sit on a well-worn love seat.

"Would you like some tea?" Claire asked as she

heaped the books and bears in the middle of an already-piled-up desk.

"I don't want to be any trouble."

"No trouble. I always have a little tea after singing. John is giving me voice lessons, the dear thing, but I'm afraid it's a losing battle. I'm seriously tone-deaf. Still, singing gives me joy—if I don't have an audience."

As she'd talked, she'd bustled about the office and in no time had produced two china cups of steaming herbal tea from a kettle on a hot plate atop the file cabinet. After she handed Kitt her cup, Sister Claire settled on the couch beside her. She lit a small white candle on the coffee table, then turned a smile on Kitt.

"What do you do for a living, Kitt?" she asked.

"I'm a lawyer, a lobbyist actually," Kitt answered, but saw no relevance.

"A lawyer. Uh-huh." The sister nodded, sipped her tea. "So. What can I help you with tonight?"

Kitt didn't know where to begin, but she had made up her mind that no matter what, she would not run away this time. "I don't know, exactly. I...I just know I need help, or something. I came back to you because, well, because you're the first one I told about—you know—"

"About your baby."

"Yes, and I...I don't know. It's funny that you

said shadow grief out there just now, because that describes what I've been going through lately. It's like there's a shadow over me. I keep thinking the way I feel lately can't have anything to do with...with what happened so long ago. But somehow I think it does.''

''I am not surprised to discover that you are a lawyer, Kitt. You seem very bright, very perceptive. I think the problem here, as in many cases like this, is that there is much left unsaid, perhaps even *undone*. Would you agree?''

Kitt wouldn't have thought so before her confrontation with Danny a few days ago. But now she was sure of it, *much left unsaid, much left undone*. She nodded and lowered her head.

''As I recall, you said one of your troubles was that you felt like you were abandoning your baby if you moved on to build a normal life, to have new relationships.''

Kitt didn't move. Had she said that?

''So do you feel, in a way, stuck?''

Kitt felt the old fear rising again, but this time it seemed stronger than ever, as if it might actually suffocate her. She threw her head back and sucked in and released a mighty draft of air. She nodded again.

Sister Claire pulled a tissue from a box, handed it to Kitt. Kitt hadn't intended to cry, but as soon as she clutched the Kleenex, tears sprang up.

Claire continued calmly. "Are you going to live the rest of your life in sackcloth and ashes?"

"I..." Kitt made a helpless motion with the Kleenex, near the area of her heart. "I don't know what to do."

"Well, let's pretend that you could write a letter to everyone you ever knew—parents, siblings, cousins, friends, co-workers, your old high-school principal—and tell everyone exactly what you did. Would that help?"

Kitt stared, openmouthed. Was this woman mocking her?

"Not practical? Not even rational?" Sister Claire mumbled, "Uh-huh," and continued. "On the other hand, you could simply decide to keep your secret and be guilty and unhappy and warped about it. You know. Punish yourself, convince yourself that because you made one mistake, you are unworthy of a future, a family, happiness, love."

Kitt's face crumpled. She bent forward and put her head in her palms. Sister Claire had given a word to the very punishment she had chosen: unworthiness. Unworthy of...no, she couldn't think about Mark, not yet.

Sister Claire leaned forward, speaking softly near Kitt's ear. "Uh-huh. So you've already taken that option. I've seen that one many times." Kitt lowered her hands and looked into sympathetic eyes, shining like stars in the soft light.

Kitt straightened and pressed her fingers to her lips. "This sounds so crazy, but I think I've even lost my true love because of this…this unworthiness." She continued in a whisper, through her fingers, as if wanting to hold back the awful words. "The irony is, he…he's raising his child, a four-year-old, but I couldn't tell him about mine."

Sister Claire's eyebrows shot up.

"I thought that would doom our relationship…that our pasts, our choices, were irreconcilable. I thought he wouldn't love me if he knew…" Kitt said this last with a cry. She put her hands back over her eyes. Would anyone ever believe the story of her and Mark, of such an incredible coincidence?

But Sister Claire responded calmly. "That's what unworthiness does to us. It makes us think we can never overcome our mistakes. It's a great destroyer."

Kitt nodded, stared straight ahead. "I broke up with Mark. And ever since I broke up with him, I can't seem to really get past it. Right after…after the adoption…I went through a period of hating men, going after men in my work, even. When I came to see that for what it was, that it was making me bitter, I started going to church again. It was like I thought by being good, throwing myself into good works, I could atone for my mistakes…and then I met Mark."

Kitt tilted her head up and stared at the crown molding, but in her mind she was seeing Mark, seeing herself with Mark, seeing how good it was to be in love.

"We only went out together a few weeks, but he made falling in love so easy!" She laid her head back on the couch. "It was like I was happy for the first time in my life. I just can't forget him. But I just keep thinking if he ever found out what I've done…" She felt Sister Claire's encouraging clasp on her forearm. "Don't you see?" She squeezed her eyes shut.

Sister Claire gripped Kitt's arm tighter, as if to strengthen her. "Yes. I do see. But I wonder if you see."

Kitt opened her eyes.

"If you want to feel truly loved and accepted in that relationship, you will eventually have to tell him."

Kitt looked at the sister, who smiled before she continued. "But whether you choose to tell this man or not, there's a lot of healing to do here. You must forgive yourself, forgive the father of your baby. And you must let your baby go. That's the way to peace, Kitt. When you find peace, you will be released from this feeling of unworthiness. And you might even be able to tell Mark the truth."

Kitt frowned and shook her head. "It's too late for that."

Claire squeezed Kitt's arm again. "Nevertheless, you must take some concrete steps to help yourself."

Kitt looked Sister Claire in the eye, nodded firmly.

"Good. Now, as a first step—" Sister Claire's voice shifted suddenly, becoming lower, almost hypnotic "—I want you to just get in touch with the feelings you have about your baby."

The resolve that had filled Kitt only a millisecond before fled at this simple request, and a great spike of fear lanced through her.

"Close your eyes if it helps," Sister Claire instructed.

Kitt managed it, reluctantly. Then she gasped. Because what she saw, bathed in a brilliant white light, was a baby's face with eyes closed. The old image from her nightmare.

Kitt opened her eyes, seeking escape, but it was too late, the image had come, and her eyes filled with tears because of it. She turned and tried to focus on the sister, whose own eyes were closed.

"Close your eyes, Kitt," Sister Claire repeated without opening her own fully.

Kitt faced forward and had to press her fingers over her eyes to keep them closed, and her fingertips and face were suddenly slick, oily with tears. Her slender arms and shoulders began to tremble.

"What do you feel? What do you see?" Sister said calmly.

Kitt concentrated on the backs of her eyelids as if they were a movie screen, the need to answer the question momentarily calming her. "My baby. Floating...sleeping, I think," she said.

Ever so quietly, ever so gently, Sister instructed her, "I want you to imagine the baby as a four-year-old, safe and happy."

Kitt turned away, eyes squeezed shut. She shook her head. "I don't think I can," she whispered. "I always see him as helpless, floating away."

"But the truth is, he is a growing child, with his parents, with his family. You are forgetting that you are the one who is feeling the loss, not him."

Kitt opened her eyes, stunned. Sister Claire was right. Kitt's baby wasn't a helpless infant anymore. Her son was a growing child—Tanni's age, in fact.

At that moment Kitt felt as if she had become suspended. She couldn't express any of this to the sister. She could only bite her lip, hugging herself, eyes squeezed shut, as she clung to that image. Her baby—her four-year-old son—was safe.

They sat together in silence on the sagging office couch for a long time while the candle burned low and Kitt quietly cried herself out.

Finally Sister Claire covered one of Kitt's hands with her delicate, warm one.

"You know what, Kitt?" the older woman said.

"Sometimes after people have imagined their child, I suggest that it's helpful to give the child a name."

This surprised Kitt. "A name?" she said, wiping at her cheeks.

"Yes. Sometimes it helps. But think about it for a while before you do." Claire smiled, and pulled a fresh tissue from the box, which Kitt took as a signal that their session was almost over. "And leave the rest to God. God is ever so good at healing even the deepest hurts."

Kitt blew her nose on the tissue and smiled back at Sister, feeling suddenly light and very glad that she had decided to come to this woman. "Thank you for seeing me."

Sister Claire nodded and sprang off the couch. "You're quite welcome." She opened the door. "If you want to see me again, I'll be here. For now, Kitt, go in peace."

And, amazingly, mysteriously, miraculously, for the first time in over four years, Katherine Louise "Kitt" Stevens did go...in complete peace.

CHAPTER NINETEEN

IT HAD JUMPED OUT at her as if it had been inscribed there, waiting for all time. She looked up the meanings, both literal and interpretive, and her choice was certain. The name she chose meant Messenger of Truth.

The distinguished-looking gentleman behind the jewelry counter seemed curious, but trying hard not to show it, trying hard to be solicitous. "This name alone on the one side?" he'd said as he scanned the little slip of paper through his bifocals.

"Yes," Kitt had answered.

She had been to five jewelry stores before she found the perfect locket on the perfect chain. A heart-shaped locket of purest gold. A chain that was delicate yet strong, like the hold this child had on her heart.

"Eighteen-carat gold," the man had assured her as he removed the locket from the lighted case and handed it over for approval. "A real treasure."

It felt warm in her palm.

But when she told him to discard the picture-holder and then gave him the small slip of paper, instructing him how to inscribe the inside covers, the gentleman had been unable to suppress a discreet frown. A hint of pity flickered across his eyes as he read the words. "All right, ma'am," he'd said, looking kindly at her over the half glasses. "Exactly these words?"

"Exactly those words."

IN THE DAYS AND WEEKS that followed, Kitt wore the locket around her neck at all times, touched it frequently. She felt renewed energy and enthusiasm for her work.

She went back to see Sister Claire a few times. Each time the healer led Kitt through another short guided-imagery experience.

Their last visit was in late March, and Kitt brought the locket. Sister Claire lifted it gently, held it close to her bifocals to read the tiny inscriptions inside, then nodded approvingly, solemnly, as she handed it back to Kitt.

"I'll never forget you," Kitt told Claire. "You are the one who helped me to heal."

"Not I." Sister Claire smiled.

Kitt confessed to Claire that day that she felt that in some ways her life was still incomplete. She started to say something more about Mark, but decided there was nothing to say—he was, after all, in the past. Kitt had learned well by then how incredibly intuitive Claire was, and she did not mistake the meaning in the nun's expectant raised eyebrow.

"May I pray for you before you go?" Sister Claire said. And she prayed for Kitt, right there on the little couch. "Please show Kitt the way of true love," was all she said.

Kitt's heart contracted at those words, but then she thought if she believed in God, surely she could believe in love. She thanked Claire and pressed a fat envelope into her hand. "It's cash," she explained. "I...I guess it seems crass, but it's all I could think of."

Sister Claire only smiled as she thumbed through the stack of bills. "So, is this how you lobbyists do it?" She winked, then slipped the envelope into the pocket of her jogging suit without further ceremony. "Thank you," she said. "I know several elderly folks who can use a boost."

When Sister Claire gave Kitt a goodbye hug at the door, she repeated what she had told Kitt that first night. "Remember, God is ever so good at healing."

KITT FELT HERSELF growing stronger each day after that. The gray guilt that had once enshrouded her life was gradually lifting. And one day she realized she had finished with the crying, finished with living in the past. And one night as she drifted into sleep she realized that the old nightmare had not troubled her in a long, long time.

And then the letter from Mark arrived.

It came on a perfect day in late May, a day when sunshine, sweetness and renewal permeated even the humid, polluted air inside the Washington Beltway.

When she got home from work, Kitt left the front door standing open to allow the remaining evening sunlight to flood the tiny foyer. When she found the letter on the table, she stood there in the slanting rays for a long time, staring at the bold block handwriting. And her fingers automatically went to her locket.

From the small kitchen at the back of the town house, she heard Lauren call out, "Kitt? That you?"

"Yes! I'm home," Kitt answered brightly, but hearing the strain in her own voice, she decided to retreat to her room to read the letter in private.

Dear Kitt,

Long time no see. Well, I guess you're wondering why I would write a letter to you after all this time. It's the craziest thing. It seems I got another internship—just a brief one for four weeks—in D.C. this summer, and I was wondering if I could come by and see you while I'm up there and bring you something. Carly has some videotapes she's been meaning to send to you. Right up your alley. She said the coalition could use them. She wants me to bring them to you. I could bring them to your house. Or I could deliver them to your office. I'll call you when I get to D.C. to see which arrangement is agreeable to you.

> Yours,
> Mark

She stared at the word *yours* as if its meaning were literal. He was not hers, and he would probably realize that after he heard what she had to say. She knew that Claire was right. She would have to tell him if she wanted complete peace, complete release.

She reread the letter.

The choppy style was not at all Mark's. She supposed he'd been first ludicrously breezy and then stiffly formal because he was, like her, very much afraid. Afraid of how this would be received, this news out of the blue. He was giving her an out. No big deal if you don't want to see me, it said between the lines.

But she did want to see him. She wanted to see him more than she had ever wanted to see anyone in her whole life. She touched the locket again. At last, she was ready to see Mark. She only hoped that Mark was ready to hear what she had to say.

CHAPTER TWENTY

"MARK, COULD WE *please* get out of this stinking...graveyard?"

Mark dragged his attention from the packages in
the meat cooler up to Carly, who stood behind him,
gripping the handle of the grocery cart, the look on
her face one of staunch disgust.

"Carly, I told you, you have to feed Tanni some
chicken and fish while I'm gone. I don't want my
kid eating off the bottom of the food chain for four
weeks." He returned his attention to the packages of
chicken breasts—so damn expensive!—but Tanni
would never eat the less pricey cuts of dark meat.

He sighed. He was tense enough about leaving
Tanni in Carly's care, alone in Oklahoma. He sure
didn't want to have to contemplate things like lack
of protein in addition to all of his other worries.

"You know, you're getting more like Dad every
day," Carly sniffed. "In fact, Dad may actually be
more tolerant than you are."

"Then maybe you'd like to go back to California,

back to *Dad,* Miss Holier-Than-Thou-Sprout-Eating Fanatic!'' He said it too loudly, too vehemently.

Carly blinked then looked around to see if other shoppers in the vicinity had noticed Mark's outburst. Then her expression hardened into genuine ire as she fixed her gaze on Mark.

Mark ignored Carly's scrutiny and turned back to the meat cooler. He hadn't meant to snap at Carly. Without Carly here in Oklahoma he wouldn't have survived. In fact, even *with* her generous help, there had been times when he thought he was losing his mind. Between cramming for his upper-level journalism classes, writing for the *Oklahoma Daily* and the *Dallas Morning News,* scrounging up money, hustling for internships and raising Tanni, he was a little stretched. Hell, he was microscopic copper wire.

Then there was Kitt—or the memory of her. He rubbed his forehead as he studied the ridiculous prices on the meat again. *Don't.* Do not think about Kitt. For the thousandth time, he wished he'd never met Kitt Stevens, for he knew with certainty that for the rest of his life, every other woman would pale by comparison.

He snatched up four packages of the chicken breasts, and turned to toss them in the basket, which wasn't there. Carly had quietly disappeared. She did that a lot lately, in response to his stupid outbursts.

He carried the packages of chicken to the produce aisle.

"Carly, I'm sorry," he said when he found her. "I know I've been kind of edgy lately." He laid the chicken in the basket.

"Lately? You've been edgy ever since you sold that precious motor scooter." *And even edgier since Christmas,* she didn't add. Whatever had happened between him and Kitt Stevens while she and Tanni were in Carmel hadn't been good, she knew that much. She could tell by the way he bit his lip when she and Tanni opened their gifts from Kitt. Carly felt vaguely guilty about the whole thing. She probably shouldn't have written to Kitt. But, my gosh, the man needed help.

"I know I've been a pain," Mark was saying, "but it has nothing to do with selling the Kawasaki, and it has nothing to do with you. Okay? Hey, let me make it up to you. Whatdaya say?"

Carly smiled her best Masters smile. "Oh-kaay. All is forgiven, brother dear—" she tossed her long black hair over her shoulder "—*if* you'll go to church with me and Tanni before you leave on Sunday."

Mark groaned, then grinned. Carly the Relentless. "Okay, but don't get any ideas. Just because I go doesn't mean I've changed my mind about organized religion."

Carly nodded. "Understood," she said. She frowned thoughtfully and pointed at him with an ear of corn. "Listen, as long as you're acting halfway decent, there is one more favor you could do for me."

"What?" he said, already suspicious.

"Would you take something to Kitt Stevens for me while you're in Washington?" Carly turned to the corn bin and picked up another ear, examined it nonchalantly, as if what she'd requested was nothing extraordinary, as if they hadn't avoided even so much as the mention of Kitt's name for the last five months.

"Kitt Stevens?" Mark said, feeling his face heat up.

"You know, that lawyer you dated, the one that went to my church? You know, the one who gave Tanni that little statue—"

"Yeah, I know." He was feeling a funny pressure in his chest, having trouble keeping his breathing steady.

"Well, I want to send her some tapes…and it'd be so much easier if I didn't have to pack them up and mail them. And cheaper. And safer. You know how mail gets lost in D.C. all the time. Would you just take them to her for me?" Carly remained focused on the corn, pawing through the bin.

"Carly, I thought I asked you not to maintain contact with Kitt Stevens." Mark felt his heart racing.

Carly proceeded to stuff her corn into a plastic bag, "I didn't, okay? I just…I just happen to know she'd want these videotapes, okay? We talked about them. For the uh…the whatchamacallit…the archives at the CRM."

She dropped the corn in the basket and plunked her hands on her hips. "Look, would you just do it? I could call her and tell her you're coming or…" Carly shrugged, turned away and ran her hand over some nearby eggplants. "Maybe *you* could…you know, write a little letter to her yourself, or e-mail her or something. You know, to save us the long-distance charges."

Mark rubbed his forehead again, tried to maintain a frown, but couldn't hold out against the goofy grin Carly shot over her shoulder. "Okay," he relented. "Just a note."

"Just a note" had sounded so simple when he'd agreed to Carly's request. So why did he stay up until the wee hours, taking forever to write and rewrite a one-paragraph letter that read like a sixth-grader had written it.

CHAPTER TWENTY-ONE

MARK HAD BEEN PARKED on the street for what seemed hours, watching as the moon rose, white and thin. It hovered above the trees, stealing across the faces of the town houses like a thief. Finally, its beams lit the alcove of Kitt's front door, and still she had not come home.

Where could she be, he wondered, out so late? On a date?

This thought made him wish he could break into her house and erase his asinine message off her answering machine: *Kitt, it's me, Mark. Well, uh, I'm here in D.C. I'll just run those tapes by, uh, while I've got a car. I borrowed one from a friend—a car, that is—* Mercifully, the machine had cut him off.

Good job, Masters. Inviting yourself over. How lame. But he couldn't wait another minute to see her.

As his plane had taxied into National Airport, he had looked out his window and seen, beyond the immense new construction, a Metro train sluicing by on the tracks above, moaning as it headed south. And he felt as if his heart was pulled by that train down into Alexandria, where he knew she was.

He'd wasted no time when he got to the rooms at American University. He borrowed a car from a friend he'd made last summer, found a pay phone and left that dumb message. Now he sat alone in the moonlit shadows on her street.

He rolled down the window and breathed deep. The night air was heavy with the fragrance of box-wood—a fragrance Kitt loved, a fragrance she had taught him to love. He whispered "Kitt" just for the pleasure of her name, then he laid his head back against the headrest as despair washed over him.

What was he doing here? Was this some kind of sick need with him? To get rejected by Kitt Stevens every six months or so? But of all the women he'd dated since Christmas—and there'd been several—not one face came clearly to mind.

On the seat next to him were the tapes. Once he gave them to her, accomplished his phony task, then what? It had been a mistake to come directly here, first thing. He was shooting his wad. He should have talked to her on the phone first, maybe enticed her to go to lunch with him or something.

Deciding to leave, he sighed and reached to start the engine. Then he heard their voices. The three women were talking, laughing, walking down the dark sidewalk directly toward him. He picked out

Kitt's silhouette immediately, panicked, then realized she wouldn't recognize the borrowed car, probably couldn't even see him sitting there, with the moon reflecting off the windshield.

The women crossed the street two parking spaces in front of him. Peripherally, he noted the tiny round form of Lauren and the tall lanky frame of Paige, but he kept his eyes on Kitt, only Kitt. She was wearing a pale-colored pantsuit and to him, she looked a little thin.

They clustered on the narrow brick steps in front of their town house while Paige unlocked the door. The sound of Kitt's laughter floated across the street, and his heart felt as if it had been physically squeezed.

He sat there, thinking what to do, watching the changing patterns of the lights in the windows of the town house while the moon moved on.

Then he thought, *Oh, to hell with it,* grabbed the tapes, bolted from the car, marched across the street and punched the doorbell decisively. The sidelights flared yellow, and Mark could feel himself being scrutinized through the peephole.

The door flew open and there, framed by the warm white interior of the entry hall, stood Kitt. Her face, even cast in shadow, looked radiant. Her hair shone like a golden nebula around her head and shoulders.

"Mark?" she said, obviously surprised, smiling a little uncertainly.

Oh no, Mark thought. What if she hadn't listened to her answering machine yet?

"Hi. Uh, hi, Kitt. I'm sorry I didn't call first. Actually, I did call—did you check your answering machine? Since I got the use of a car tonight, I thought, well, I'd better bring these on over." He thrust the tapes toward her, then senselessly pulled them back. "Did I disturb you or something? So late, I mean? May I come in?" *Keep babbling, Masters. That's always impressive.*

"Well…"

Damn! She was hesitating. He shouldn't have come. He *knew* he shouldn't have come.

"I need to check with Lauren and Paige first. It *is* late. I think they're already in their robes—" She herself stood there in some kind of full, flowing thing, all soft pinks. "Let me ask if they mind. Wait here."

The door closed and he was left on the stoop, a lone figure on the dark street. Only then did he think to check his watch by the sidelight. Eleven o'clock! Good grief. She must think him a moron, dropping by at this hour.

The door flew open again. "Come in," Kitt said, then looked down and stood aside.

He stepped into her home, passing within inches

of her, so close that he could breathe her perfume, and he immediately knew, with all the certainty of all lovers, that she was still The One. God help him, he was in the presence of Kitt. He studied her profile as she closed the door. She had removed all traces of makeup. *God,* he'd forgotten how beautiful she was. No he hadn't. He'd just forgotten how beautiful she was *in the flesh.* If she touched him, he would go to pieces. Joy and fear mixed like drugs in his blood.

She turned and smiled at him. "Well," she said brightly. "Here you are!"

"Yes. Here I am. And thank you," he said. "Thank you for letting me in." He could have cheerfully slapped the inanity out of himself, but instead he smiled lamely.

"Would you like some hot tea?" she offered, all perfect poise. "I was just brewing some. Or does something cold sound better?"

"Uh. The tea sounds nice."

He followed her to the kitchen at the back.

It was a small, narrow room with a rear wall of wavy paned windows that looked out on a tiny moonlit courtyard at the back of the town house. The room smelled of something freshly baked and had the feeling of being overgrown with houseplants.

"Neat plants," Mark said.

Kitt smiled and a warm familiar look passed over

her eyes that almost undid him. "Yes, they're…neat. They're Lauren's," she added. He thought she was going to say something else, but she pushed her bangs out of her eyes and turned to the cabinet and took down two tea mugs instead.

He seated himself at the small breakfast table.

When she bent forward to pour the tea, he noticed the locket between her breasts. He'd considered buying her a gold locket once—he'd even gone so far as to ask her if she had one—back when they were first dating, but that was before he'd severed from his father, before he began selling all his worldly goods to survive. Now he didn't have the money to buy a locket. Was there some guy in her life who *did* have the money?

"So, how've you been?" he asked, trying to sound casual.

"Fine." She smiled at him, added honey to his tea.

"And everybody else? Lauren and Paige? Eric?"

"They're fine." She stirred the tea. "Lauren and Eric are seeing a lot of each other these days."

"That's nice," he said. "And, uh…how's Jeff?"

A tiny crease formed between her eyebrows as she set the mug in front of him. "Jeff's fine. But he's been working too hard lately." She seated herself, then stirred her own tea. "How're Carly and…Tanni?" she said.

"They're great. Just great. Tanni's in kindergarten now. Smart as a whip. Draws the cutest things. Carly still doesn't know what she wants to do with her life."

"Is she planning to take some college classes?"

"Oh, sure." Mark reached over and rubbed the glossy leaf of a nearby plant between thumb and fingers. "She just doesn't know when or where or what. I'm going to have to sit down with her and help her make some plans." He smiled, and when he looked up, he saw that she was watching his fingers as he rubbed the leaf. Her lips were parted slightly—and she seemed mesmerized by the action of his fingers. Suddenly the kitchen seemed too close, too warm, too brightly lit. She raised her eyes to his and when their gazes locked, his fingers stilled on the leaf, tingling, tingling, and the quiet around them seemed like a physical thing, swirling, swirling. The blood pounded in his ears. He couldn't sit here and make chitchat and pretend. He had to say it.

"Kitt," he said in a husky voice, fingers still touching the leaf, eyes still on hers. "God help me...but I still love you."

She looked away, swallowed, and for a moment seemed unable to speak, unable even to blink. He waited, his heart pounding. He steepled his hands in front of him, pressed his forefingers to his lips, watching her for any sign. Then she said, "Mark, before you say anything else, I have to tell you something," and her hand went to that locket.

His heart sank. He closed his eyes, thinking that he already knew what it was she had to say—that she'd found someone else—and wondering how in God's name he could sit here and listen to that.

"Mark, please look at me," she said.

He opened his eyes, lowered his hands, tried to arrange his large arms on the narrow table in what he hoped was an attentive-but-not-tense posture. She still clutched the locket. Her green eyes, even devoid of makeup, were incredibly beautiful, and they were sad now, wide with dread.

Don't cry here, Masters, he thought. *It will only make this worse for her.* He squinted with the effort of restraint. Inside him, a battle raged. Will versus feelings.

"Go ahead." His voice cracked when he said it.

Kitt nodded, tight-lipped. Inside her a battle also raged. Courage versus fear. He deserved to know, didn't he? Isn't that what she had decided when she got his letter? To tell him at the first opportunity, so he would understand and be truly free. Kitt closed her eyes, summoning determination, and began.

"Mark, something happened to me this past winter, just before Christmas—well, no, actually something happened to me about five years ago—" She stopped.

How could she say this? The image she had seen with Sister Claire came back to her—her baby was safe—and that idea gave her strength. She opened her eyes, looked into his, which were inscrutable, and began again.

"Mark, once, years ago—five years now, to be exact—I was in love with someone else. His name was Danny. He was funny and smart and really good-looking." She gripped her tea mug with one hand and rubbed the locket with the other.

Mark stared at the locket. *And now this guy's back in your life,* he thought.

"We were both from small towns, in law school together at O.U. We had the same friends. We had so much in common. And we…we had a brief affair—"

Mark looked down at his arms. He didn't really need to know anything about her past to know that he loved her. Why was she telling him this? Unless it was for the obvious reason: this Danny guy was the one who was keeping them apart.

"I just assumed the commitment was there for both of us. We never really talked about marriage. We were concentrating on law school." She closed her eyes and drew a mighty, shuddering breath.

But now you have *talked about marriage,* Mark thought.

"But then I got…pregnant—" The word *pregnant*

came out in a pained whisper. "And right at the same time, I found out that Danny wasn't as committed as I thought he was. He was…he had been sleeping with other women all along."

Mark frowned, blinked, struggled to process this unexpected information. *Pregnant?* And the guy was sleeping with other women?

He looked up at Kitt as an expression of horror formed on his face, then quickly hardened into rage. Whoever the hell this Danny was, Mark had the sudden urge to beat the crap out of him.

Kitt saw the change in Mark's expression. She mistook it for anger at *her,* for her deception. Her face crumpled as great tears of fear sprang to her eyes, but she fought them back, determined to finish. Having finally said this much of it, she felt a burning desire to tell the whole story before she lost her courage. "I was scared, I guess. Scared of raising a child alone. Scared of losing a career I hadn't even launched yet. Scared of humiliating my family. Scared—"

Her voice broke, and she drew another shuddering breath. "I hate to admit how shallow I was, but I was afraid of ending up stuck out on that farm with my father, raising a child—but I think mostly I was afraid of somehow being tied to a creep like Danny."

Kitt gulped and tears started to course down her cheeks. She was rubbing the locket with an agitation that Mark was now beginning to understand. "I was so terrified of that, that I didn't want anyone, not anyone, to ever know..." She said this last in a small, frightened voice that tore at Mark's heart.

"So I...I did a...a cowardly thing—" it seemed to Mark that Kitt was having trouble breathing. "I..." she continued haltingly "...I gave my baby up for adoption."

Mark started forward in his chair but she raised a palm to stop him.

She took another gulping breath, lowered her palm, swallowed again. "But it's okay. Now I truly feel I've made peace with myself. I've even made peace with the baby. Now I just want to make peace with you, too. I know that sounds crazy, but I truly feel that my baby, *my baby*—"

She clutched the locket and held it forward as if it explained something, but then she seemed unable to say more. She threw her head down on her arms and succumbed to sobs.

Mark stood. He looked down at the top of Kitt's head. Then he slowly grasped her shoulders with his big hands and drew her to a standing position in front of him. He cupped a finger under her chin and caught one tear off the edge of her jaw, tilting her face up to his own. "My God, that's the secret you've been keeping," he whispered just before he brought his mouth down on hers. "And I thought I'd lost you forever."

CHAPTER TWENTY-TWO

IN THAT ONE INSTANT, that one kiss seemed to obliterate their long months of separation. Kitt tilted her head back, giving herself over to him.

Mark groaned and pulled her tighter. As always, the fit of her slender body to his muscular one had a symmetry, a communication, all its own. He wanted to have this wondrous feeling—the feeling of holding Kitt Stevens in his arms—all the days of his life.

After a long time of tasting, renewing, tasting and renewing, he broke the kiss, drew a deep breath, looked in her eyes and said, "Why didn't you tell me about this sooner?"

Kitt closed her eyes. "I was afraid."

"Afraid?"

"Yes. Of what you'd think of me. I was afraid you'd think I was awful...for giving my child away."

"Why would I think that?"

"Because you have Tanni."

Mark swallowed, understanding all of it now. "I only have Tanni because of my mother's help and my father's money. Don't you see? You did the best you could, Kitt.''

Before she could respond to that he went on, his chest tightening. ''For a minute there, I thought you were going to say that you'd found someone else.''

Kitt's mouth dropped into a soft O of realization, and he covered it with a tender kiss.

They stopped again, only because looking into each other's eyes seemed even more fulfilling. ''There could never be anyone else,'' Kitt said. ''Not when I love you so much.''

Mark let out a sudden joyous whoop, and grabbed her to him, swinging her up off her feet, whirling her around in the small kitchen. ''She loves me!'' he hollered.

''Shh!'' She slapped at his shoulder. ''Lauren and Paige.''

''Oh yeah,'' he whispered. ''Let's go someplace where we can talk and make out. I want to touch you all night long.''

AFTER KITT CHANGED into jeans and a sweatshirt, they took the car he'd borrowed and drove to Founders Park by the Potomac. The full May moon shimmered across the water, blending with the reflected lights of Strand Street. They strolled along the river, holding hands, clasping arms around each other's waists as if they'd never been apart. Kitt told him more about her baby than she had ever shared with any other human being. She told him about her sessions with Sister Claire. And she showed him the locket. Mark stroked her hair while she shared these things. Then he kissed the locket. He didn't ask her for details about the father of the baby.

Eventually they stopped beside a picnic table on the waterfront. Mark lifted Kitt up onto the tabletop, facing him, and positioned himself between her legs. Then, with his hands cupped possessively around her hips, he gave her a very slow, very sultry kiss.

"This kissing is going to get us in trouble sooner or later," he said huskily. "So I expect we'd better go on ahead and get hitched."

"California boys should never attempt an Okie accent."

"Well, then, like, let's do the marriage thing."

"You're serious?"

"I love you."

"And I love you." She pressed two tiny, soft kisses to his jaw. "But don't you think this is a little sudden? Don't you think we should give your family, Tanni and—and your father especially—time to get used to the idea?"

Mark huffed. "My father. I could bean that old man. For a while I wondered if his behavior at the Fourth of July picnic was the reason you had bolted from our relationship. I wouldn't blame anyone who didn't want to get involved with the Masters dynasty. But fortunately for us, my father is not running my life anymore.''

''I can't believe you gave the CRM the money from the sale of your Masters Multimedia stock.''

''I wanted to help you, but more than that, I wanted to be free of him. I know it seems crazy, but I'm starting out like any other middle-class guy in America, and it feels great.''

''Your dad will come around eventually.''

''And what if he doesn't? Do you care?''

Kitt shook her head. ''All I care about is you, and Tanni and Carly.''

''They're crazy about you.''

''But even so, a child needs time to get used to the idea that she's going to have a new mother.'' Kitt pressed her fingers to his lips so she could keep talking. ''You know, Mark, I didn't think I could be a good mother to Tanni, not after I had given up my own child. And I didn't think you'd want someone who had made such a selfish decision to be Tanni's mother.''

''Kitt. No.'' He pulled her head down to his shoulder and she threw her arms around his neck and hugged him tight. ''What you did wasn't selfish.''

She released a huge sigh. ''God! I was scared of what you'd think of me when you found out,'' she confessed.

"Shh." He stroked her hair. "Don't talk about it anymore. I think you're wonderful, just like I always did. You and Tanni will get along great. She needs a mother. She needs *you*."

"And I need her," Kitt said with tears of love in her eyes. "She's such a beautiful child. She's almost the exact age—"

"I already figured that out, sweetheart. Promise me something." He gave her a soft, reverent kiss on the forehead. "Promise nothing will ever come between us ever again. No more secrets."

Kitt nodded.

"Now answer my question, will you marry me?"

"You are the only man in all the world I would ever say yes to."

This time when he kissed her, it felt like their first kiss in Dumbarton Oaks all over again. Like floodgates opening. Tasting him and feeling his power, his passion, filled Kitt with joy, and she felt almost light-headed, remembering the crazy way in which they had started.

A giggle bubbled up at the memory.

"What's so funny?" he said.

"Before we get married, I think I want to enjoy the experience of dating."

"Dating?"

"Yeah. You know, dates," she teased, using his

exact words. "Movies. Dinners. Walks in Dumbarton Oaks."

Mark sighed, catching on. "Okay, I guess I can wait while we do a little more of the dating thing, but it's going to be *hard*."

"Stop that." Kitt slapped his shoulder.

"Kiss me."

AT THE END OF Mark's summer internship, he announced that he would take Kitt on "one last date."

"Wear that peachy-colored thing," he said.

When he pulled up to the parking spaces on R Street across from the old iron gates, Kitt knew exactly where Mark was taking her. And she knew why. And she knew that this time she would give him an unbridled yes.

Inside Dumbarton Oaks, they strolled along the narrow paths, down over the terraced gardens, past the mighty oaks, until they arrived at last to a small plateau, above a cool, inviting lagoon. "Lover's Lane Pool" where tall silver maples whispered in a protective ring around a shallow stone pond. Where the treetops created an elliptical window of late-afternoon sky reflecting on the glassy green surface. Where Mark and Kitt had first kissed.

Mark took her hand as he led her wordlessly down the steep path and Kitt's heart started to pound. This was the moment she had thought would never come.

The moment when she not only believed in true love, she felt like the embodiment of it. Sister Claire had been right after all. "Thank you," Kitt whispered toward the sky.

"What?" Mark turned his head absently.

"Nothing."

"I want us to be in the exact spot," he said, and pulled her along until they arrived at the heart of the setting.

ON THE HILL above Lover's Lane Pool, a mother and a father and their cranky ten-year-old son climbed the path in the July heat. At the top, they stopped to catch their breaths and marvel at the beauty surrounding them.

"Like stepping out of the noisy city into another time," the father commented. "Too bad we got here so late in the day." He checked his watch. "They close at six."

"Yes," the mother sighed, examining her map. "We can't see all of this in only one hour."

"Then let's *go,*" the ten-year-old boy whined. "This is just a bunch of flowers and bushes and stuff, anyway."

"Here, Nathan," the father handed the boy a video camera. "Occupy yourself filming something."

The boy ran ahead of his parents, then stood in

the center of the brick path, videotaping the scene below, snickering.

"Oh, look." The mother came up beside her husband and pointed at the apex of the pool below, where a young man wearing a dark suit knelt on one knee before a young woman wearing a flowing peach-colored dress. The man was holding one of the woman's hands in both of his own. "How sweet."

"Nathan, I hope you aren't filming those people." The father rushed forward and put a hand on the boy's shoulder. "That is obviously a private moment."

"I bet it's some kind of joke. That lady's laughing."

"It's rude to videotape people without permission," the father insisted.

But the mother was frowning. The young woman's shoulders did appear to be shaking, and her head was thrown back, but she thought perhaps that instead of laughing, the lady was crying. She tugged at the boy's arm. "Turn the camera off." They turned their backs to go back up the path.

Just then the young man below them whooped and the distant sound echoed off the water, the stones, the trees. As the little family turned toward the noise, the man rose from bended knee and hugged the woman fiercely, sweeping her up and whirling her around and around.

The dappled evening light played over the couple like the lights of a thousand tiny diamonds and the boy said, "Wow!" as he smashed the camera back up to his eye.

"Nathan," the father warned.

"Hey!" The boy lowered the camera. "I saw something shiny fly away! I did, Dad! I saw it flash!"

"Nathan, let's go. *Now.*"

An hour later, just before the six o'clock closing time, the family circled back by another path to Lovers' Lane Pool. The young couple was nowhere in sight.

The boy was kicking along the path, still in his disgruntled mood, when suddenly he became agitated, "Hey!" he yelled. "Hey!" He held up something shiny for his parents. "Look what I found!" He ran to his father holding out a small gold heart-shaped locket on a broken gossamer chain.

"I'll be," the father said.

"I bet it was that lady's!" The boy grew more excited. "I was right! Something shiny *did* fly off her neck when that guy was whirling her around."

"Maybe we can find them," the mother said.

"Wow," the boy said. "This is real gold, isn't it, Dad?"

"Let me see it." The mother held out her hand.

The family crowded close to see what was inside the locket as the mother carefully pried it open.

Inside, in bold letters, was inscribed a name, JOSHUA, and below that the words *my baby* in minuscule script. Engraved on the other side was an epitaph in the same delicate script.

The father took it from the mother and pushed his glasses down on his nose. "It says, *When my father and my mother forsake me, then the Lord will take me up. Psalm 27.*"

The boy wrinkled his nose. "What the heck does that mean?"

"Only the rightful owner of this locket knows." The father looked pensive. "But I'll bet this thing has great sentimental value."

"Maybe we can give it back to her." The mother scanned the surrounding terraces for sight of the couple.

But it was late and the young couple was long gone.

Indeed, the family had to hurry back to the main gate. It was already a little past six.

At the gate, they tried to give the locket to the guard, but the old fellow refused to accept it. "I don't have nowhere to put it and the docent ladies are all gone," he explained.

A few weeks later, when vacation memories were fading, the mother found her son watching the videotape, alone in the den, freezing the frame at the exact point where the tiny speck of light had spun into the air.

"Do you still feel funny about that locket?" the mother said, staring at the blurred image on the screen: a beautiful, slender blond woman in a peach-colored dress, her head thrown back, her eyes closed in ecstasy, elevated in the arms of a strong young man in a dark suit. She was touched by the joy that was so evident in the faces, the bodies, the embrace of the couple. The tiny particle of brilliant light, the locket, had already spun far to the right, the young woman innocent of its trajectory.

The boy looked at his hands, rubbing a dirt smudge listlessly. "It's too bad that lady lost her locket and we could never find her," he said.

"I'm sure the lady has gotten over losing it by now," the mother reassured her son. "Why don't you erase that piece of tape, honey? After all, we don't even know those people." She had given the locket to her mother's rabbi weeks earlier. "Use it for the poor," she had said. The young woman's loss was sad, but, after all, it was not the end of the world. Life goes on.

EPILOGUE

Seven years later

KITT AND MARK STOPPED frequently as they climbed the winding path, adjusting the baby stroller: the awning, the cotton blankets, the tilt of the seat. The gravel on the path made the going bumpy and the baby got fussy. Finally, Mark stopped the stroller, reached in and lifted his son out and snuggled him up against his broad shoulder.

"Maybe it was too hot for him in that thing," Kitt said, and smiled up at Mark as he patted the baby's back.

"Or maybe he's just a lot like his old man, and likes to be held." Then he cocked a dark eyebrow at her, as if that had reminded him of something. "He'll be thirstier in this heat. Did we bring a water bottle?"

Kitt squinted down the shadowed footpath below. An arch of huge trees prevented her from seeing far. "The girls have it in the diaper bag. Where did they go?"

Mark stepped back to her, took her elbow gently with his free hand. "Tanni took Carrie to the bathroom. They'll be along soon. Come on."

"But children are supposed to be accompanied by an adult in the gardens. What if Carrie touches the plants? You know how she is."

"And you know how Tanni is," the father said. "Big sister will not brook any misbehavior. Come on—" he tugged at her elbow again "—let's find a place to feed this guy. He's about to suck the blood outta my neck."

Kitt smiled. The baby was rooting on Mark's neck like a fat little piggy. She didn't think she'd ever seen such a vigorous, healthy baby. She reached up and cupped her hand around his perfectly shaped head, relishing the silky feel of his dark curls.

They made their way up the path and Mark spotted an iron gate standing ajar. Inside it, a wooden bench sat back among some high boxwood hedges. Below the shady plateau where the bench sat, tubs of gardenias, lantana and citrus made the air rich with fragrance. "In here, sweetheart," he said. "This spot is secluded."

The baby was starting to fuss in earnest now, and Kitt quickly abandoned the stroller, sat down on the bench, pulled aside her soft knit blouse and bra, and laid a light blanket across her shoulder. Then she raised her arms to receive her son.

"Oh my goodness," she cooed as the searching little mouth immediately fastened. "We are a thirsty boy. Ah!" She caught her breath at the force of the baby's sucking, at the sudden letdown of milk.

"No one has to tell this guy what to do," Mark said as he parked the stroller out of the way. Then he settled himself on the bench next to them and smiled that smile that Kitt loved.

Mark took in the sight of his wife and his son, adoring them as one unit.

Kitt's breast was a creamy orb, echoed by the baby's fat little cheek. Her hair fell across the side of her face like a soft curtain, on which the dappled light, coming through the trees above, created pools of topaz, the exact shade of her hair that he loved.

"I love you, Kitt," he said. She smiled. At the baby, not at him, but Mark knew her smile was for him, too, reflected off his son.

"Where are those girls?" Kitt worried, looking up from the baby.

Mark stood, craning his neck to peer over the hedges, and shading his eyes as he surveyed the sloping terraces below them. "I see them," he said. "Tanni's dragging Carrie by the hand, up that brick path down there. They'll be here in a bit."

"Tanni is so responsible for an eleven-year-old," Kitt said. "Do you think we expect too much of her?"

"No. She's just like you." His eyes sparked with pride. "There's no such thing as too much responsibility, never too big a challenge."

"Oh, there can be too big a challenge for me. I probably should have stopped the consulting when I found out I was pregnant again," Kitt sighed. "Sometimes I get so tired. And I feel like I haven't really talked to you in weeks."

He sat back down on the bench, reached behind her neck and massaged.

"Part of it is having to make this trip to D.C. so soon after having the baby," he reassured her. "Let's just relax and take this chance to visit for a minute, okay? This is our family day. You don't have to go back to the capitol until tomorrow."

"Thank God," Kitt said, and relaxed her head against his comforting hand.

He lifted her hair off her neck and blew gently, causing a tiny thrill to ripple down her shoulders and spine.

"Is it okay with you that we brought them here?"

"The girls? Absolutely! I want them to see where their daddy proposed to me."

"Well, it *is* a special place for us." He resumed his massaging. "And Tanni's always been curious about it, hearing the story of the romantic proposal at Dumbarton Oaks, ever since she was four..." His hand paused. "But I was just thinking...wondering…I hope…I hope coming back here doesn't make you…you know, kind of sad, too…''

"You mean, because this is where I lost the locket?" Kitt said.

She got a faraway look in her eyes and he leaned forward, studying her face as if trying to read the feelings there, the memories.

"Kitt, are you thinking of—" He stopped. He looked so concerned that it nearly broke Kitt's heart. They hadn't mentioned it again since that day when they'd hurried back to the gardens to search for the locket, finding the gates already shut. After she'd called the docents the third time, she had finally accepted that the locket was truly lost.

And then they'd gone back to Oklahoma, to Tanni. Had a wedding, built new careers, houses, gardens, raised horses, dogs, more children. But always, Kitt remembered.

She moved her hand from the baby's back and touched the delicate gold chain that held the locket Mark had bought her as a wedding gift.

Mark watched her hand as it caressed the new locket, the one engraved with their names and their wedding date, then he looked at their baby briefly, then up into Kitt's eyes. A crease formed between his thick eyebrows and he chewed his upper lip.

"You're wondering if I was thinking of Joshua?"

she said calmly. Then she looked down at the baby at her breast. "Yes, I was. I was thinking of him."

"Oh, sweetheart," Mark said, and moved closer to her on the bench, encircling her and the baby gently in his arms, those wonderful arms that were like a haven to her.

It seemed easy for a tear to come when everything else was flowing anyway, and Mark scooped it off her cheek, then kissed it off his finger, a gesture he'd adopted all those years ago. A gesture she cherished. After a while he said, "Maybe coming here was a bad idea." He searched her eyes. "I mean, you're still postpartum and all."

She smiled. Mark was amazing.

"I'm okay. Really. Sometimes it's good to remember, you know. To think about how far I've come."

"I'm really proud of you, sweetheart." He brushed her bangs out of her eyes for her. "Not many people could run a lobbying consulting business while raising a family."

"I couldn't do it if you weren't willing to stay home with the kids when I have to travel."

Mark shrugged. "Hey. I can write feature stories anywhere. And LinkServe is LinkServe is LinkServe. What kind of CEO would I be if I didn't run it from my home office? *Anywhere You Are*, the old LinkServe motto."

"Aren't you glad your dad talked you into taking it back?" Kitt had asked this question many times over the years. But in quiet moments, they enjoyed reminding each other of the many changes that love had wrought.

"Yeah." He gave her a little squeeze before he released her. "I'm glad I listened to my smart wife and gave the old man another chance. Especially after Carly moved back to Carmel."

"I think your dad is as proud of the work she's doing with disabled children as Carly is."

The voices of the girls drifted up to them from the path beyond the hedges, and Mark stood and waved his arms over his head. "Tanni!" he called. "Up here!"

And then they flew around the hedge, breathless from running the rest of the way up the hill. An eleven-year-old and a four-year-old, so imprinted with their father's dark good looks that no one would ever guess they had different mothers.

They flopped down on the grass in front of the bench and both parents smiled indulgently at their daughters.

"Mom!" the older one complained. "Carrie takes about *forever* to wash her hands!"

"I do not!" the four-year-old retorted. "I do it zactly the way Daddy taught me."

Kitt gave Mark a grin. "And I always blamed Carly for that."

"For what?" Tanni asked, straightening and sitting cross-legged in front of her mother.

"For teaching you—" Kitt touched the tip of Tanni's freckled nose lightly "—to wash your hands as if you were scrubbing for surgery. You were so cute that time I took you to the rest room at First Baptist."

"Oh yeah!" Tanni laughed, "I remember. The time you found me in the big church. I was just about your age, squirt." Tanni poked Carrie, who cuffed her in return, then started rhythmically jabbing her big sister's knee.

"*Carolyn,*" Mark warned before a tussle developed.

"Where was that church, Mom?" Tanni asked, ignoring her younger sister's jabs.

"Not too far from here. In Alexandria," Kitt said.

"Daddy, I want to see the 'posal place," Carrie whined.

"The baby's not through nursing yet. Maybe Tanni will take you on down and you girls can wait for us there. See the path?" He pointed for Tanni. "It's that shallow pool and amphitheater down there. We can watch you from here." Tanni jumped to her feet. "Come on, squirt." She extended a hand to her sister, then pulled her to her feet.

The girls ran off, their voices and laughter echoing off the canopy of trees overhead.

"I want just a few more minutes alone with you," Mark said as he settled back on the bench. He lifted her free hand off the baby and kissed it, first on her knuckles, then he turned it over and kissed her palm.

Kitt studied the top of his head as he did this. He was so beautiful. She sighed, rested her head contentedly against the high back of the bench. Then she giggled.

"What?" He looked up, curious.

"Oh, nothing," she said dreamily. "I was just remembering the first time you kissed my hand. It was right here. At Dumbarton Oaks." She gave another small chuckle and the baby sighed against her breast and then fell away from the nipple, his rosy mouth slack with contentment and sleep. "Remember that?"

"I kissed your hand? Here? Madam, methinks you are imagining things."

She leveled a knowing smile at him. "I thought you were so cute."

"You thought I was so *nuts,*" he retorted.

"Well, maybe your advances were a little…"

"Asinine?" Mark supplied.

"Offbeat." Kitt grinned. "Oh, but you were so *wonderful,*" she said.

She'd said *wonderful* with a touch of Oklahoma

accent that drew out the word so that the mere sound had actually stirred Mark's loins. It had always been like that with her. Just a word, a look, a touch, and he wanted her.

He kissed her hand again. "So were you, babydoll, and you still are." He pushed the baby blanket on her shoulder aside, admiring her bare shoulder and breast. "And you still are," he repeated in a husky whisper.

"You know that I want you right this minute," she whispered back as he covered her and then folded her and the baby in his arms again, guiding her head into the hollow of his shoulder.

"I want you, too," he said, and kissed her forehead. "And as soon as your body's able, I'm going to show you just how much."

Kitt closed her eyes and breathed in the smell of his neck—so pure, so healthy, so male.

"For now, a kiss'll have to do," he murmured, slanting his mouth over hers.

They kissed then, their mouths meeting directly over the baby's sleeping head, their hearts beating in unison against his sturdy body. Three lives in a sunny garden, twined in joy.

Presenting...

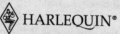
HARLEQUIN®

PRESCRIPTION
ROMANCE
Rx

Get swept away by
these warmhearted romances
featuring dedicated doctors
and nurses.

LOVE IS JUST
A HEARTBEAT AWAY!

Available in December
at your favorite retail outlet:

SEVENTH DAUGHTER
by Gill Sanderson
A MILLENNIUM MIRACLE
by Josie Metcalfe
BACHELOR CURE
by Marion Lennox
HER PASSION FOR DR. JONES
by Lillian Darcy

Look for more
Prescription Romances
coming in April 2001.

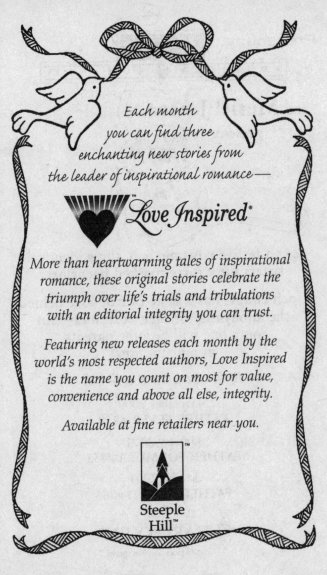

Each month
you can find three
enchanting new stories from
the leader of inspirational romance—

Love Inspired®

More than heartwarming tales of inspirational romance, these original stories celebrate the triumph over life's trials and tribulations with an editorial integrity you can trust.

Featuring new releases each month by the world's most respected authors, Love Inspired is the name you count on most for value, convenience and above all else, integrity.

Available at fine retailers near you.

Steeple Hill™

HARLEQUIN

AMERICAN ◆ ROMANCE

and Muriel Jensen

present

WHO'S THE DADDY?

*A*t a festive costume ball, three identical sisters meet three masked bachelors.

*E*ach couple has a taste of true love behind the anonymity of their costumes—but only one will become parents in nine months!

Find out who it will be!

November 2000
FATHER FEVER #858

January 2001
FATHER FORMULA #855

March 2001
FATHER FOUND #866

HARLEQUIN®

*M*akes any time special ™

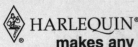

Tyler Brides

It happened one weekend...

Quinn and Molly Spencer are delighted to accept three bookings for their newly opened B&B, Breakfast Inn Bed, located in America's favorite hometown, Tyler, Wisconsin.

But Gina Santori is anything but thrilled to discover her best friend has tricked her into sharing a room with the man who broke her heart eight years ago....

And Delia Mayhew can hardly believe that she's gotten herself locked in the Breakfast Inn Bed basement with the sexiest man in America.

Then there's Rebecca Salter. She's turned up at the Inn in her wedding gown. Minus her groom.

Come home to Tyler for three delightful novellas by three of your favorite authors: Kristine Rolofson, Heather MacAllister and Jacqueline Diamond.

HARLEQUIN®
Makes any time special ™

PHTB